The Dream and the Muse

Jake Burnett

SOUTH
WINDOW
PRESS

You see the world the way you are.

- Mouldywarp

Printed in the United States of America

First Printing, 2021

ISBN 978-1-7346642-4-9

South Window Press
P.O. Box 6573
Raleigh, NC 27628

www.southwindowpress.com

Cover design: Rocío Martín Osuna

1.

The full moon scowled like a skull through bone trees. Madarena Rua glared back. She'd been trying to sleep for hours. As if the blazing white light flooding through her window weren't bad enough, her father's snore echoed all the way down the hall.

Sneeee... whonnnkkk... gurggg... sneee... whonk... gurggg...

She had no idea how her mother slept with all that ruckus right next to her head. Madarena had no plans on marrying. Ever. She didn't like anyone. And even if there were anyone she liked — even in the *extremely* unlikely event she found someone tolerable enough to be around all day, who could stand the night-time noise?

She flipped her fake-feather pillow over her face. She pressed it down tight across her eyes. She stuffed the pillowcase into her ears. It shut out the moon and the snores. Wrapped in a cocoon of darkness and quiet, she almost drifted off.

Until her stupid dependence on oxygen ruined it. She flung the pillow to the floor and gasped for air.

"Feh!"

(She'd heard an old man say that in the library once, when he was informed they didn't have the book he wanted. It struck her as the perfect word for very many frustrations.)

She stared at the network of branch shadows on her ceiling. Boredom crept round the edge of her bed. She had to act quick before it could climb in.

She sat up. She squinted across the room at her desk. Her dictionary lay on her desk, open to the IMs where she'd left off.

"You…" she muttered at the moon. "Impious celestial body."

The massive four-volume set had been the one thing she'd requested for her birthday.

Wouldn't you like some clothes? Something more fashionable than the shabby three things you insist on rotating through?

No, Mother. I would not.

What are we going to do with you, child?

She'd gotten clothes too. An utterly impractical collection of garments that demanded matching and forethought. She stuck with her standard, whenever she could. Black tights, knee-length purple turtleneck dress, raggedy flannel hoodie over the top. The hoodie was the differentiator. She had three colors.

Disreputable, her mother called it. A time-saver, Madarena countered. The argument recurred.

The dictionary, though. Ah! There was a present! Every word ever and their definitions *and* their histories. With examples as far back as before English was English. She needed a magnifying glass to see the tiny, tiny print.

Can't sleep, might as well read. Let's see who was the first person to use 'impossible' in a sentence.

She swung her legs to the side of the bed. A chill wafted up from the floor before her feet even touched the boards. The hairs on the back of her neck stood up. Gooseflesh crept up and down her arms.

That won't do.

She stuffed her feet back under the eiderdown. She rubbed her arms vigorously. She scanned the dim room for her slippers. She spotted one in a corner and another by the door. Neither could be reached from the warmth of the bed.

Feh.

It was her own fault. She'd kicked the slippers catawampus with a wild cry, before making her nightly running leap into bed.

"It seems," she said aloud, "we are at an impasse."

She had just learned the word and was eager to give it some air.

She cogitated on the impasse. The key objective was to avoid feetcicles. A plan took shape in her brain.

She had three pillows — one for sleeping and two silly, uncomfortable ones that her mother insisted on for 'decorative purposes'. Those two had beaded pictures of hedgehogs on them. How having your face-skin poked with beads all night was supposed to be acceptable, Madarena had never understood.

All three lay on the floor beside the bed. She retrieved them. She brushed dust off the useful pillow, fluffed it, and returned it to its proper spot. She set one of the hedgehog pillows back on the floor, bead-side down. She could just stand on it with both feet and not touch so much as a toe on the freezing floor.

Chilly but bearable.

She put the second decorative pillow a step in front of her. Transferring herself to it, she reached back for the first.

"Impasse surpassed!" (She was a long way from the SUR entries, but she could extrapolate).

Smug at her cleverness, she repeated the process till she got to the slipper in the corner. She stopped off at the closet to get her thick russet-red robe. Wrapped in wool and warmly beslippered, she booted the picture-pillows this way and that.

The first bounced off the closet and settled at the foot of her bed with a satisfying *whuff*. The instant the second pillow whuffed off her desk, though—CRASH!

Madarena leapt into bed. She pretended to have been asleep the whole time.

Sneeee… whonk… gurrrgg…

After a few of Father's snores, she realized the crash of shattering pottery hadn't come from her room. Rather, something had smashed in the garden. Therefore, she could not be responsible.

She listened hard as she could. A light breeze creaked the bare trees. Fallen leaves scuttled on cold stones. Not enough of a wind to knock over a pot. Something must be outside.

"Everyone still immured in your beds?" she whispered loud enough that Mother would only hear it if she were awake.

Her forehead furrowed. Overhearing herself, that did not sound like the right use of the word. She made a note to look it up. As much as it pained her to have new words grow dusty unused in her brain, she hated misusing one even more.

Scraaaaape… hrrrn…

The sound of another flower pot nearly being knocked over, then caught, chased off word-worry. Curiosity even made her ignore cold feet as she pit-patted to the window.

The garden below was grey and winter-dead and filled with strange-angled shadows. Madarena stared, lost for a moment in the colorless weirdness of the moon-washed world.

A small black shape prowled down the white gravel path to the fence hedges.

Poor cat! He must be so cold!

Quick as she could while still being ghostly quiet, Madarena hurried downstairs.

When she stepped out into the frigid night, she saw at once the source of the earlier crash. One of her mother's flower pots — empty, of course — had been knocked off its low wall and shattered on the pavers below.

"Clumsy cat," she called across the yard. "Mother won't let you in the house if she finds out about that."

The cat must have heard her, because he froze in his tracks.

"Don't worry. We'll blame it on the wind."

Not assured, the cat sprinted across the garden. To Madarena's shock, he appeared to be running on his two hind legs. Before she could think what that might mean, he reached the edge of the garden. He leaped head-first into the hedges.

"Wait!"

She ran after.

As she approached, muffled spits and mutters came from the thrashing thorn bush. She stopped short.

"Mreow?"

The spits and mutters cut short. The bush stopped moving.

"Mreow," came the entirely unfeline reply.

Madarena put her hands on her hips.

"You're not fooling anyone, whoever you are. You may as well come out."

"There is nothing," a strained voice said from the hedge, "I would rather do. As it stands, I am impaled on a number of prickers. Imbowered. Immobile. Impeded in my forward progress beyond even my considerable and oft-proved ability to struggle through circumstance."

Grateful she'd reached the IMs, Madarena translated.

"You're stuck."

"Of course I'm stuck, you imbecile!" The hedge resumed thrashing.

She hunkered down. She peered into the thicket of thorns. What she saw made her blink twice and stumble back.

"How implausible!"

She really was getting to use all her new words.

2.

Tangled in the thicket was a wee old man in a shaggy grey overcoat. He appeared human in every particular except size, which was about that of a hedgehog. His nose protruded somewhat further than one might consider conventional. Glistening scratches hash-marked his bald pate. Grey wisps of hair circled its crown in disarray. He had a pot belly and spindly limbs. His bushy eyebrows beetled over glittering black eyes.

"Implausible? IMPLAUSIBLE?! That's your best epithet?!"

He frowned at her fiercely. Had he been full-sized, she surely would've been afraid. As it was, she couldn't help laugh at his tiny splayed rage.

He laughed back. His stern face crinkled till it became downright kindly. His giggle made her laugh harder, which sent him into a guffaw. This escalated until a storm of mirth swept them both helplessly away. Peals rippled across the dead garden, disturbing the leaf dust and new-formed frost.

"Well," Madarena gasped at last, "I suppose I'm going to wake up any minute now."

What else, she reckoned, could explain it?

"That's a shame. All good things end, I suppose." The wee man wiggled the hedge. "Before you go, do you think you could help an old dream out?"

"Of course!"

She reached into the thicket, slow so as to avoid thorns. When her hand closed around him, pain stabbed her palm. She yanked her hand out, raking angry scratches down her arm.

"Imprecation!" she had the presence of mind to yell instead of swearing. She shook her fingers and blew on her palm. Droplets of blood welled up from a dozen punctures.

"Watch the coat. I ought to have mentioned that."

"You're lucky I'm tough. A weaker woman would've woken up when you stabbed her."

"I have come to rely on possessing more than my fair share of luck, 'tis true."

Madarena inspected him. The overcoat that she'd thought was shaggy grey wool was, in fact, composed of layer upon layer of quills — like a hedgehog's spiky skin.

"Tricky."

The little man watched her expectantly. She considered going to the shed for a rake, discarding the notion almost at once.

"It'd probably just poke you in there further. Or maybe run you through."

"I do not know what you were thinking." The man furrowed his beetle-brows. "Perhaps another round of planning is in order."

"Eureka!"

"Melodrama!"

"Shush."

"Fum. Fuss."

She took off her russet robe. Shaking with cold, she pushed the robe into the hedge. She wrapped it around the quill-coat. Thus protected from the prickers, she extricated him with one hard tug, quick as a cork from a jug. She shook out the robe. He spilled undignified to the ground.

"Brrrr… Wake up soon, Madarena." She huddled her robe back on. She bounced up and down to get warm.

The old man kipped up with surprising agility.

"Much better." He patted himself all over. "Much."

He squinted up at Madarena, who towered over him.

"This disadvantage won't do. At all."

His moonshadow stretched wide and tall from his feet. He raised his hands over his head, like a gymnast. He rocked on his heels. He rolled forward until he nearly fell onto his bulbous belly. Just before he hit the ground, he tucked into a somersault.

So quick Madarena could not follow, the wee man tumbled head-over-heels *through* his own shadow. When he landed upright on the other side, he stood the same height as the shadow — a few centimeters taller than she.

He bowed.

"Apophax, forever in your debt."

"Madarena Rua. No worries."

His sudden transformation did not startle her, of course. These things happened all the time in dreams.

Apophax smoothed his ruffled comb-over. He rubbed his hands together.

"So, Miss Rua. Since you do not seem to be waking up any time soon, would you care to join me on my preaubadal perambulation?"

She puzzled over the last two words. It didn't seem right that her dream used words she didn't know. Before she could ask, he explained:

"A walk before dawn. I'm new to the area and a guide is always welcome."

"Why not."

As she led him to the garden gate, she repeated 'preaubadal perambulation' several times. If she could remember them after she woke, she could skip to the Ps and figure out which one meant 'walk' and which 'before dawn.'

Out in the street, Apophax glanced left and right. Not finding what he was looking for, he asked: "What do you call this place?"

"Sentinel Street?"

"No, no." He waved his hands wide as he could. "Think more grandly. Live beyond the streets you call home. What do you call the whole entirety of it all?"

"The world? It's just… the world."

"The world…"

Apophax stared far between the stars. Madarena recognized his expression. Her mother often corrected her for 'blanking out' when all she was doing was flipping through her brain-files for some bit of memory.

"The world." This time he said it firmly, as if he'd figured something out. "More than your fair share of luck…" he murmured to himself.

"What?"

From the front of her parents' house, a dog barked three times.

Apophax's long nose twitched. He tapped it.

"Is there a cemetery within a brisk stroll of this boulevard?"

"A cemetery?"

"You know the word implausible, yet stumble over cemetery? You're a curious woman, Madarena Rua."

A low growl crawled over the roof of the house across the street. As if the dog perched on the dormers. Apophax's words hastened their pace.

"A graveyard. Burying spot. Ossuarium. A soily repository in which the recently deceased gather to become the not-so-recently deceased. A—"

"I know what a cemetery is."

"And? Is there one nearby"

"There's one on Peabody and Church."

"Does it have a gate?"

"Of-of c-c-c-ourse it does." Her teeth chattered. The chill had settled in. She wished she'd wake soon. Her bed was warm and this dream had gotten tedious.

The wind whirled up. It shivered her to her core. A third dog barked thrice. Apophax's black eyes glittered in the bright moonlight. Cunning fluttered across his face.

"My goodness! Poor thing, you must be so cold! Here."

With a gallant flourish of his wrist, he stripped his quill-coat off. He draped it over her shoulders.

"Put this on. Warm yourself up."

"Th-th-th." Her jaw quivered too hard to thank him properly.

"On, on. There you go."

She slipped her arms through the sleeves. They hung loose on her wrists. Apophax tugged at the cuffs. The coat resized to fit her as if bespoke. She warmed up at once.

Apophax looked her up and down.

"The spit and image."

Another dog—Madarena couldn't remember there being this many noisy hounds in the neighborhood— sounded off loudly, right round the corner. The old man's eyes darted in that direction.

"Terribly sorry." Something about the way he said that gave her shivers all over again, from the inside out this time. The moon grinned down on them and the Man in the Moon had never looked more like a skull.

"What for?"

"It's you or me, you see. You seem nice enough, it's just that I am ever so much fonder of me. I'm sure you'd do the same."

He took a careful step away from her. Madarena blinked. The tricky moonlight made it look like he was fading.

"What are you talking about?"

"Nothing at all." His voice dropped to a hoarse whisper. "Just the ramblings of a dream, right?"

With that, he paced slowly across the street. With each step, he grew paler and dimmer, until he was the exact shade of the moon-bleached street.

"Wait! What about your coat?"

Madarena tried to take it off, only to find she couldn't. She yanked the sleeves and tore at the collar. The hedgehog coat would not be removed.

She ran to the empty space that had been Apophax seconds earlier. He was truly gone. Vanished into thin, chill air. She stood alone with only her shadow for company.

At her back, something growled low and stalked with clawed feet across the asphalt.

3.

She didn't want to turn around. But not knowing was always worse than knowing. So she turned around.

A tall creature, white as bones, strode straight towards her. It had the body of a strong man and the head of a lean and hungry dog. Its bare feet ended in leonine claws. It wore a long tunic the same color as its skin. It made her think of an Egyptian marble statue from the museum, come to life. Anubis, his name was.

Two meters from her, it stopped. It raised one hand, index finger pointed.

"Apophax."

Its voice was dry as dust in a desert that had never drunk rain.

Madarena squeaked. She leaped, turning full about-face as she jumped. She ran full tilt down the street.

A cloud of dust swirled past her. The smell of chalk itched her nose. The swirl coalesced in her path—the dog-headed monster.

"Apophax. You have broken the laws of Triskadeka Fair. Prepare —"

She didn't wait for it to finish. She spun on her heel. She feinted a few steps down the street. When the dust brushed her neck, she spun back round and took off in the other direction.

It did not work.

"Apophax," the Anubis said a third time. Its tone never once changed. Madarena had never heard a voice so dry.

"I'm not—hurp!"

It seized her. It hoisted her over its shoulder. It was not in the least bothered by the spines of the quill-coat.

"You have broken the laws of Triskadeka Fair. Prepare to climb the Lichgate Stair. Judgment has not been passed. Judgment will be fast and just. Ashes to ashes. Dust to dust."

It said no more.

It carried her down Sentinel Street. Turned left on Church Street. Loped on with a steady stride.

The whole way, Madarena struggled against its grip, to no avail. She wiggled and she wriggled and she flexed every muscle she had. She beat its broad shoulders — that just hurt her fists. She bit one pointy jackal ear and nearly chipped a tooth.

By the time they'd reached Peabody Avenue, she realized force would not help. She tried reason.

"I'm not Apophax. He just gave me his coat. We can discuss this."

She wouldn't bet much money on that approach. Reason nearly never worked with anyone else, why should dog-men kidnappers be any different?

To her surprise, the walking, talking rock set her down. They stood at the burying grounds. Staring at the sidewalk to better concentrate, she marshalled her arguments.

"Right! Let's talk this thr —" she looked up "— WHAT IS THAT?!"

A long stairway made of solid moonbeams rose from the cemetery gate. It ascended as far as she could see — kilometers into the air, if her eyes could be trusted.

"Apophax, you are ordered to climb the Lichgate Stair."

"Are you always this implacable?"

Using one of her new words right shored her up. Made her braver. Reminded her she was smart, maybe smart enough to find a way out of this nightmare.

The Anubis folded his arms across his chest. One white fang poked out from his sneering alabaster lip.

"Alright, alright. I'll step on the moonbeams and you'll see that I'm not Apophax when I fall through. And you'll be hearing from my attorney about this."

The first stair glowed, translucent. She could see the cemetery dirt below. Light bathed her slipper. She stepped.

It held.

Solid as stone.

In wonder, she forgot all about the menacing statue who'd forced her onto the Lichgate Stair. She climbed upwards. Her heart raced and her head buzzed.

With every step, the Earth dwindled beneath her. After ten steps, she could see the curve of the horizon. Ten more steps and the whole world had shrunk to the size of her parents' house. Thirty steps up, it looked no bigger than the globe in her father's home office. Forty steps up, she could've picked up the whole planet and popped it in her mouth like a gumball.

By the time she reached the hundredth stair, all the people alive and dead, all the history and animals and plants and oceans and clouds and skyscrapers and wars and hate and love and books—all of everything that everyone said was so important—all of that couldn't be found amid a sea of pinpoint stars.

At the top of the moonbeam staircase, completely incongruously, she found a stout oak door. It bore a sign:

COURTROOM 1-C: *Apophax v. Triskadeka Fair (et al.)*

Madarena took one last, long look into the endless spread of outer space. She hoped she would remember the sight after she woke. Or at least carry that feeling with her into daytime life.

She set her shoulders. She prepared for a fight.

"Alright. Let's clear this impropriety up."

She pushed the door open and stepped through.

4.

Another Anubis — this one a woman — waited within.

"Your Honor, the accused, Apophax of Oneiros."

Madarena stepped into a small office, painted a dingy institutional grey. The statue closed the door behind her with an ominously understated *click*. The only other exits were doors on the right and left, marked 'Guilty' and 'Innocent' respectively. A fourth door, no taller than Madarena's ring finger, exited through the far wall.

A small grey metal chair sat in front of a grey metal table. On either side of the table stood a little desk ornament with raised letters made of scuffed tin. The one on her side read ACCUSED and the one on the other side JUDGE.

The judge waited, sitting. A grey robe covered her—or him or them—head-to-toe. A deep-cowled hood hid their face. Trumpet sleeves swallowed up both hands.

"Bailiff, if you please," a stern, high-pitched voice ordered from within the cowl. It sounded as if it came through a long tin tube. "Let's get this conviction started."

"Oy!"

Madarena did not know much about the law, despite her lawyer father's best efforts, but she knew a trial was called a trial and *not* a conviction.

"The Accused will be silent until called upon. The Accused will be seated for judgment. Judgment will be fast and just. Ashes to ashes, dust to dust."

"I got that part already," Madarena muttered, taking her seat.

The Bailiff set a silver tablet and a keyboard in front of the Judge. The Judge tapped the screen. It made a gavel sound.

"Apophax of Oneiros, you stand acc—"

"Objection!"

"On what grounds?"

Madarena blinked. She hadn't thought that would work. "On the grounds of me not being Apophax. Also, I'm sitting. So I can't stand accused."

She winced. That was a dumb thing to add.

In the event, it didn't matter.

"Overruled. As are any other objections you may register, so stop wasting the court's time."

Madarena snorted. "Seriously? Are you all blind? Look at me! I'm a young woman. Apophax is ancient! And a man."

The judge stabbed the tablet rapidly, drowning Madarena out with gavel sounds. Madarena could not be so easily squelched. Many had tried.

"He's bald! BALD!" She shook her thick unruly mane at the judge. "Does this look like a wig to you?"

"Bailiff, restrain the Accused!"

"Mrphpmhpmrhm." Madarena grumbled a few choice imprecations into the Bailiff's stone hand over her mouth before settling down. The Bailiff let her go.

The Judge typed three hundred words a minute, *tika taka tika taka tika taka.*

"This court does not recognize insanity pleas. No one in the Quaquaversal judiciary does, Apophax. So you may as well give it up. Pretending to be mad is not a valid legal strategy for these proceedings. Your insolence, however, has been duly recorded."

Madarena folded her arms over her chest. "This court doesn't recognize insanity pleas because this court is crazier than a soup sandwich."

The Bailiff moved towards her. The Judge raised a hand, stopping her. *Tika taka tika taka.*

"By all means, Apophax. Continue. I've added a contempt charge for that last comment and am more than happy to tack on a few more."

"I have not yet begun to contempt."

Tika taka tika taka.

Madarena bit the inside of her cheek (a trick she'd often used when she had more to say but saying more would only make things worse).

"With no further interruptions from the Accused, this court proceeds to the indictment."

In a tinny monotone, the Judge read charges from the tablet. They paused every so often to swipe to a new screen.

Apophax's crimes required a great many swipes. Worse, by the time the Judge finished (nearly an hour later), a grim suspicion grew in Madarena's belly.

She was not dreaming. This was real.

The main clue:

The indictment was full of words like 'egression' and 'inculpatory' and 'transmigration'. Words that Madarena knew she'd never heard nor read. She had never made up words while dreaming. She did not think it was likely she would start.

Which left only a very discomforting conclusion.

"…and an additional charge of contempt of court added during the course of the initial indictment," the Judge wrapped up. "How does the Accused plead?"

Madarena knew the drill. Another question that wasn't a question and whose answer would change nothing.

"It is beneath my dignity to plead."

"And it is beneath the dignity of the court to laugh at your petty, obstreperous efforts to evade your fate. However, I am willing to grant a scoffing noise."

The judge emitted a metallic *scoff*.

"Do you have any case to present other than nonsense about mistaken identity?"

So many pointless questions. Madarena uttered an imprecation, without replacing it by 'imprecation.' She did tack on a 'your Honor.'

"I thought not. This court finds you guilty."

DONK!

The tin letters in front of her reshaped themselves from ACCUSED to CONVICTED.

Madarena slumped in her chair. She'd been in more or less this position most of her life—not in an official court, of course. She and implacable authority had never once met in the middle.

"Given the severity of the charges and the Convict's complete refusal to admit culpability, this court sentences Apophax the Oneiron to be bound in the Triskadeka Jail until such time as he is consumed by remorse. Sign here to accept the verdict and sentence."

The judge flattened the tablet and pushed it across the table. Madarena frisbeed it back at their head. The Bailiff snatched it out of the air. She grabbed Madarena's index finger. She dragged it along the surface in a rough facsimile of APOPHAX.

"Court is adjourned." *DONK!* "Bailiff, take the defendant away."

The judge slumped face-first onto the table.

"Oy!" Madarena shoved her chair back.

A small lump wriggled down the trumpet sleeve of the judicial robe. Out of the hand-hole came a tiny grey-skinned woman, slightly stooped over. Her iron-grey hair was pulled back into a tight bun. She had six arms and two legs. She glared up at Madarena through a pair of glasses with sixteen lenses.

"I hope remorse eats you quickly, you insolent scofflaw." Her voice piped small and high—near inaudible without the amplifier in the Judge suit. "I've never tried a more recalcitrant defendant."

Discombobulated by the judge's weird appearance, Madarena couldn't even process the new word.

With that, the judge-bug scuttled off the table. She climbed deftly down the metal leg. She left by the tiny door in the far wall, which opened and closed automatically.

Flummoxed, Madarena allowed herself to be guided by the shoulders through the 'Guilty' door. Utterly befuddled, she made no protest as the Bailiff led her down a long flight of poorly lit steps, round the curve of an ill-smelling tunnel, to an iron-banded door. She was still trying to make sense of what she'd just seen as the Anubis pushed her into the cell.

The sepulchral slam of the prison door snapped her out of confusion.

By then, it was too late to do anything.

"Until consumed by remorse."

Gritty footfalls receded.

Cold radiated from the stones of the cell. Dust and must and smell of long-forgotten bones filled her nose. What had begun as a seed of suspicion bloomed into certainty. There would be no waking up.

"Right," she firmly ordered herself. "The important thing is not to panic."

Whereupon, she panicked.

5.

She screamed.

She pounded on the door. She scrabbled the walls. She stamped the floor. She ran in tight circles, windmilling her arms and wailing. She shouted threats and imprecations and bargains, not knowing if anyone heard nor if anyone cared.

Eventually, she exhausted herself and her options.

She sucked in jagged breaths until her heart stopped pounding and her lungs released their iron grip on the inside of her chest.

Time to take stock of her situation.

She paced three long steps from door to wall. Two steps from side to side. That was her cell.

A small barred window, above head height, let in cold bluish-white light. A small pallet on an iron rack shoved hard against one wall. A hole in the opposite corner (much too small to crawl through) provided a place to do the needful.

Scriiiitch. Scriiiitch.

Following the sound, she found a pile of bones beneath the mold-stinking cot. Only the 27 bones of one hand were still assembled. Beneath the tip of the outstretched index finger, scratched into the grey stone floor, white letters read:

REMO

The distal phalanx had worn down to nearly a chip — as if the digit's previous owner had kept scraping the floor long after the flesh pad had scoured off. The finger twitched.

"Oy!"

Her back hit the dungeon wall.

Scriiiiitch. Scriiiitch.

It didn't leap out and throttle her. Might as well figure out what it was doing — since she was trapped in here with it for the foreseeable future.

She lifted the mattress to better let in the light. The skeletal hand moved with agonizing slowness. It traced the same shape, over and over and over. Ever so faint in the stone, Madarena made out another 'R' next to the final 'O.'

Until consumed by Remorse.

The judge's sentence might, in this lunatic prison, be brutally literal.

"Nothing to it. I'll be fine. What do I have to be remorseful for?"

She would've preferred her voice not tremble so. The point of talking aloud was to shore herself up, not drive home her fear.

"Feh!"

That was better. It was hard to say the word "feh" fearfully. She said it a few more times. She dropped the mattress. She rubbed her hands together. Her shadow, stretched across the floor and halfway up the door, caught her eye.

That's odd.

Its limbs looked spindly. Not like her own at all. She turned sideways. An enormous pot-belly protruded from the shadow.

Double odd.

She ruffled her hair into a mad halo.

The shadow's head cut a smooth black circle on the wall. With an improbably long nose.

Odd to the oddth. With a side of deep weird.

To her own eyes, in the flesh, she appeared as she always did. The shadow was unquestionably Apophax's.

Explains why everyone thinks I'm him. Sort of. Not really. It just kicks the mystery up a level. Feh.

While she knew she had no real hope of solving the puzzle right then, she welcomed the distraction from the skeletal hand and the ominous fragment REMO.

She took a step into the corner. Facing the ceiling, she cupped a palm over her ear. She did her best impression of Apophax.

"I seem to be impaled on a number of prickers."

The echo *almost* sounded like the treacherous old man. She could not be sure.

It logically must. Otherwise someone would've noticed Apophax suddenly sounded like me. Unless their tiny judge ears make every big voice —

An idea interrupted her.

She measured the little hole in the corner by eye. Apophax had been near that size when they first met.

If I'm him…

It would be a gross escape route, wading through sewage and who knew what else. Still more attractive than Remorse.

She squared her heels. She lifted her arms.

Did he lift his arms? No.

She dropped them. She rocked back on her heels. She rolled forward. The instant before her shadow's belly hit the ground, she tucked into a somersault.

BOOM!

She whammed into the dungeon door.

There must have been more to the trick than the acrobatics.

She lay on her back, legs straight up against the door.

"Ow," she said, more out of habit than real hurt. "I'm all out of ideas."

Scriiiiitch… scriiiiiitch…

"Hup!"

Even without ideas, better to do any random thing than lie there listening to Remorse consume her grim cellmate.

She turned her attention to Apophax's coat. A few more futile quill-rattling contortions confirmed she could not take it off. She moved on to the pockets. There were *dozens* of them, hidden away inside and out, under quills and tatters. After half an hour, she couldn't be sure she'd found them all.

Most were empty. She lined up what little she found on the dungeon floor.

  * One nubbin of chalk.

  * One booklet with a grinning skull moon and the word PASSPORT embossed on the cover.

  * One scrap of yellowed and spotted paper, tightly folded as many times as physically possible

  * One crisp cream-colored business card, belonging to:

> *K. Landvermesser*
> *Assistant Undersecretary*
> *Interworld Property Impoundment and Return,*
> *Oneiros & Mnemosyne Division*
> *Vordem Gesetz, Logos*

She flipped open the passport. A solid block of tiny text covered the first page.

"By the Concordat of the Thirteen Worlds and the Laws of Triskadeka Fair…"

Triskadeka Fair. The Anubis said the same thing. That must be where I'm at now. I've never heard of it. I'm not impressed so far. If I get the chance, I'm leaving a scathing review.

From there it descended into a dense thicket of legal jargon. After some study, Madarena deduced the gist was that the bearer, APOPHAX, was a citizen of somewhere called Oneiros. The booklet gave him the right to travel to and from a place called Triskadeka Fair.

She would've bet her parents' house and thrown in her dictionary that it was a fake. He was that kind of crook. She weighed tossing it down the waste hole. If he were in Triskadeka Fair, he'd get in lots of trouble for not having his passport.

On the other hand, if people thought she was him…

She tucked it into the pocket of her robe — not his coat. Her mischievous chuckle drifted through the window bars.

Revenge.

The business card made little sense, even having just read the definition of 'Impoundment' that week. She memorized the name, title, and address anyway, in case it came up later.

She unfolded the compact sheet of paper. It took up half the cell. Blue pencil scribbles, circles, arrows, and a dozen other symbols covered it all the way out to the edges.

What on Earth? Or not on Earth, I guess. What on wherever? Feh. Focus!

She studied it only five minutes before she knew it had to be a Plan.

A heist. Or a con. Shenanigans, anyway.

She'd stumbled into the middle of it. She pored over the early stages, trying to piece together what had come before she'd helped Apophax out of that hedge in a regrettable act of benevolence. Strange names swarmed across the page, nestled in ovals and rectangles.

The Night Mayor. Aoede. Planck. Thanatos. Wilhelm von Katzen. Mouldywarp. Charonsferry. Pharmakos. Cosmos... some were people and some were places, of that she felt sure.

She found several names she'd already run across elsewhere. Triskadeka Fair. Oneiros. Logos.

Every time the word 'Logos' appeared, the letters squiggled, as though Apophax's hand shook when he wrote it. Next to it, as if to stiffen his resolve with mockery, he'd drawn a cartoon of a stern bug-person.

"The judge!"

Something snarly and complicated was afoot, that much she knew at a glance. Everything revolved around something named Aoede. Apophax had stolen it from someone called the Night Mayor and then lost it to the Logons. He was trying to steal her back.

That Night Mayor person showed up several times, along with what she reckoned were escape routes. The others — people and places — served some function. She could not figure what.

And always the Logons, with plot lines skirting cautiously around them.

There might be a key to the cipher on the back. She flipped the sheet over.

"Ohhhh!"

The drawing on the other side dissolved the cell around her. Staring at it, all her fear, intensity, mischief, stubbornness, and chronic dissatisfaction fell away. As if they could not stay in the same mind where that image shone.

It was a mere sketch, the lightest pencil lines in sepia, blue, and black.

It was the most real thing she'd ever seen.

It portrayed a woman, eyes downcast and closed. Her face bore an expression as distant as the farthest star. A wreath of blue roses crowned her head. Gazing at her, Madarena felt herself fade away — as though *she* were the sketch and the woman on the page was solid flesh.

A faint melody brushed the edges of Madarena's brain. Phantom music carried her to the muddled-up place where only music can take us, the place where we both are and no longer have to be so bothered about being ourselves.

"Aoede..." her whisper fell on her ears unbidden. Yes. That was the woman's name. As right as the rightest word for any thing that had a word. The music slipped into silence. In the space that remained, Madarena felt a resolve for something she could not yet name.

"Oh, Apophax. You are much too wicked for her."

Very carefully, for the sheet was worn nearly through, she folded the Plan and drawing back up. She slid off her slipper. She pried out the cushioned insole. She tucked the wad of paper safe away.

She vowed to find Aoede, to hear that music again.

Slowly, the feeling of rightness engendered by the mystical drawing faded. The disquiet of her predicament returned. She rolled the nubbin of chalk in her fingers.

What now?

Her brain said nothing in reply.

Thank you so much, stupid thing.

Nada.

She gave up. She stared off at nothing. Idly, she made little marks on the floor with the nubbin of chalk. She furrowed her brow. It looked like the start of a face. With the swoop of a mouth and an oval to frame the features, she finished the doodle.

"Hello!" the chalk face chirped.

"GAH!"

Startled, she scuffed the face into a smudge.

"Mrph. Mrphldrm. Phrmldrm."

The smudge writhed, like it was trying to reform itself. Hesitantly, she retraced the face. The mouth stretched out. It smacked thin lips.

"How rude!" it said in an aimable, if a bit thick-witted, voice. "Still, no harm done in the long run I guess. All is forgiven."

"Thank you?" She had no idea how to react. Politeness seemed a safe bet.

The dot-eyes narrowed into lines. "Who are you, then?"

"You first."

"Fair, seeing as I'm your host. The Triskadeka Jail I am and who else would I be?"

"How are you talking?"

The chalk face crinkled. The mouth squiggled like a sine wave.

"I guess I don't know. Never tried it till now. Maybe I never had nothing to say before."

"Maybe."

"Plenty of people talk to *me*."

"I believe it. I'm Mad—Apophax," she corrected at the last minute, not wanting to give her real name away. Even an affable dungeon was still a dungeon.

"Pleased to meet you, Mad Apophax." The mouth line shrunk to a dot. A little whistle filled the cell. After an awkward pause, the Jail asked: "So… what are you in for?"

Madarena remembered the interminable indictment. "Lots and lots of things."

"I'll bet! You look pretty disreputable. And I ought to know. I've seen the worst of them in my time."

"Oy!"

"No offense meant. No one's at their best by the time they get to me, are they?"

The hand bones scritched in the corner. The Jail's face twitched, like that tickled.

"How long you in for?" it asked in a 'making conversation' kind of way.

"Until consumed by Remorse."

"Oooo. Rough, that. Always hate to see that happen. Lots of screaming and carrying on and scratching my stones."

Madarena glanced at the pile of bones. She shuddered. An idea flashed across her brain. She made a show of shrugging. She kept her voice casual as she could.

"It wasn't so bad."

"Beg pardon?"

"Being consumed. I don't know why everyone goes on and on about it. I hardly noticed."

The sketch squinted at her. "You? You don't look consumed."

"Oh, that's just my exoskeleton. We Apophaxes—"

She stopped. She had no idea if he was a species. She guessed the Jail didn't either. She pressed on.

"We Apophaxes keep our bones on the outside. For convenience."

"What about that pot-belly?"

"That's... um... my... front shell!"

"Front shell?"

"Like a turtle. Except out front. So I won't get stuck on my back."

The eyes wiggled. "That *is* clever!"

"Evolution did us right." She dry-washed her hands. "Anyhoo. Enough of the biology lesson. Can you let me out?"

"Out?"

"Of course. I've been consumed, right? Except the indigestible bits."

"True..." The circle around the Jail's features zigzagged. "And now you want... out? It's never happened before."

"You're not full of bones, are you?"

"Never! They clean those out once Remorse is done."

"That proves it! Only I don't want to bother a janitor this late. Maybe you could just…"

She pointed at the window.

"Mighty thoughtful of you! Out you go!"

The door to the cell clicked. It swung open. She wondered how many doors there were between her and the street. More importantly, there were probably one or more Anubises. They wouldn't be as easy to fool.

She was going to have to be more explicit.

"The window is a better option. Closer to the trash cans, of course. And that way I won't wake anyone up rattling down the halls."

"You are so polite! I don't know why they call you Mad Apophax."

The window expanded. The lower sill reached halfway to the floor. With a screech, the iron bars pulled out of the concrete.

Madarena jumped and caught the edge. She hoisted herself up. She wriggled under the pointy bars.

"Good riddance!" the Jail cheerily called from within. "And don't do it again!"

The window snapped shut.

Madarena cackled a wild freedom laugh. She tossed the nubbin of chalk in the air and caught it. She held it twixt finger and thumb.

"Magic chalk and why not?"

She slipped it into the coat.

"Now. Let's go home. Wherever that is."

6.

Her escape went well at first.

She crawled into a narrow, empty alley. The omnipresent white glow brightened. All around, she heard the sounds of a town waking up. Quickly — though not so quickly as to attract notice — she headed through the alley.

There had to be more ways out of here than the moonlight stair. Otherwise, everyone who visited Triskadeka Fair would have to go through the Court and Jail.

Not good for tourism.

She peeked round the corner. Two Anubises stood stock-still on either side of a double door. The word JUSTICE was carved over it.

Feh. Justice.

Keeping everything except one eye and half her face hid, she watched the Anubises. They stared straight ahead. If she didn't know better, she would've figured them to be decorative statues.

I wonder if they can smell as well as dogs.

She couldn't just stroll down the promenade in the other direction. All it would take is one break in dog-headed discipline and WOOSH. Sand cloud, grabbed, back in the cell. And they'd probably figure out how she broke out. Take away the chalk.

Remorse.

She hung in painful hesitation.

A rusted pickup truck rumbled up to the alley. Brakes whined. It stopped right in front of Madarena.

Acrid blue fumes belched from the tailpipe. The muffler bounced perilously close to the road. Piles of clocks, watches, sundials, hourglasses, and sundry esoteric chronometers jangled in the bed. Digital letters on the side flashed:

J. HOURFRED PRUFTOCK

Then:

TIME IS MONEY

Then:

TIME TO TRADE

Then:

REDEMPTION CITY, CHRONOS

Then back to the beginning. Luckily, the deafening tick-tock of the idling engine covered her loud yawp of shock. Almost.

The driver locked eyes with her. He winked.

He was a tall, skinny boy made entirely of tin. His arms and legs were coiled springs. His face was circular, ringed by cog-teeth. His quartz-crystal eyes twinkled in time with his truck's engine.

With improbable precision, she knew he was exactly one year, sixty-one days, three hours, thirty-nine minutes, and eight seconds older than her.

He shoved the truck door open. Ignoring her, he marched towards the Anubises. As he passed, he pointed once, quickly, at the back of the truck. He accosted the guards, keeping their attention away from Madarena.

"I'm here to pick up the wasted time! Should I pull round back?"

She did not hear the Anubis's reply. She'd already bolted round the truck. She leapt into the back. She burrowed beneath the cacophony of clocks.

It was a split-second decision. The truck lurched forward before she had time to regret it.

She huddled, hidden, until the next time the pickup stopped. Curiosity gnawed at her, to see the sights of this strange place. Caution kept her from poking up for even a quick glance during the long, loud, bumpy ride.

The jostling stopped. A garage door slammed shut behind her. All the timepieces fell silent at once. The relentless tick-tock of the piled up clocks continued in her brain throughout the ensuing conversation.

"Twenty-seven seconds late, Planck," a clipped voice said.

Planck! From the Plan!

Madarena coiled up, ready to spring out and run away fast as she could.

"Sorry sir," came a slow and affable reply. "The Logons filed a collection order at the Jail and then when I got there the guards said they didn't know anything about it and—"

"—and nine more seconds for that excuse. Keep talking and I'll dock you. Time is money, kid."

"Yes, sir."

"Well? Don't stand around costing Mr. Pruftock even more. Redeem the time, son, redeem the time."

"Yes, sir."

Another, smaller door closed.

"Thought he'd never leave. Come on out, Mister Apophax, sir."

A tin hand swung back and forth through the mess of timepieces. Madarena took it. Planck helped her out of her hiding place.

"They weren't too rough on you, were they, sir?"

She patted herself up and down. In her best Apophax impersonation, she replied: "Not a bit of it, my lad. A veteran incarcerant like myself scarcely notices the inconvenience."

It must not have been as good an imitation as she'd hoped. Planck frowned. Only for the briefest flash, before covering it up with an earnest helpful smile.

"That's good, sir. I couldn't believe it when I saw you, I have to say. I didn't think anyone got out of the Triskadeka Jail. The Anubises and Logons keep things tight wound, everybody says."

He was talking too much and too fast. Madarena pressed the deception, channeling her best avuncular gruffness.

"Something troubling you, m'boy?"

"Oh! Sorry, Mister Apophax. It's just that, well…"

A classic way to hide shenanigans, she knew, was to make the other person feel like they were hiding something. She bristled up the coat quills. She shook her cheeks.

"Out with it! Time is money!"

That flustered him good. He stammered and looked at his feet.

"No offense, sir. It's just that, since I saw you last, you got back a lot of time. I know you didn't take it from Pruftock, on account of that would get me in all kinds of trouble, that much time missing."

"Impudence! What are you talking about?"

"You went from a few hundred hours to seventy-one years!" he blurted. He clapped both hands over his mouth. His eyes widened, mortified. "I'm so sorry, sir. I'm not supposed to say that to non-Chronons. It's just that you were yelling at me and I got nervous and I don't understand how you found all those extra years overnight."

Madarena couldn't keep up the façade any longer. Something about Planck's sincerity and kindness made her want to trust him. She wanted to trust *somebody* in this crazy place. It might as well be him.

Besides, he didn't have a lot of heft to him. She was pretty sure she could take him out and be gone by the side door before anyone was the wiser, if honesty turned out to be a mistake.

"Look. Planck is it?"

He nodded, still ashamed of himself.

"Thing is, I'm not Apophax." She raised a hand. "I know, I know. I look like him and I sound like him. That's just the stupid coat. I think."

In broad strokes, she sketched out the events of the last twelve hours. Planck listened without interruption. When she was done, he clicked his tongue thoughtfully.

"That's widdershins for sure. It does fit the extra time. And why, if you were Apophax, would you claim not to be Apophax?" He corrected himself. "Unless, of course, you were talking to the Logons. Or someone else like them."

"Is he really that great?"

"He's… great is not the word. I'm not good enough with words to find the right one."

"I have a few words for him."

"I imagine you do."

"Are you going to turn me in? Or tell Apophax? And why are you working with him anyway? You seem really nice. Is anyone actually nice?"

Planck raised his hands. "Ticks and tocks! Slow down a second, slow down. I'm still on the clock. Piles of time to redeem. I can't just drop everything and answer every question from here to eternity. Even if I knew the answers, which I probably don't."

Madarena did not object—a rarity for her, when confronted with unanswered questions. Planck had been kind to her. He didn't deserve to get in more trouble with his boss, even if he were helping Apophax.

"I understand."

She could not keep the crest from falling in her voice.

"In two hours, seventeen minutes, and change, my shift is up. When you go out to the street, take a left. Follow it for two minutes, take another left. Straight for three minutes and twenty-five seconds, not counting time spent at crosswalks. That's Orrery Square. I'll meet you there when I'm off."

"Deal." She stuck out her hand.

He was already shoulders deep in the pile of timepieces. She showed herself out the side door.

7.

She meant to go straight to the Orrery and wait till Planck joined her. She turned to the left out the door. She marched down the street for what she guessed were two minutes. Resolute, she turned left again. That was as far as she followed the tick-tock boy's directions (which, to be fair, was further than she usually followed directions).

She found herself entirely distracted by Triskadeka Fair. She strayed from street to street. She lost all track of time.

The strangest thing about the place was how familiar it all seemed. If someone had asked her to draw a town based only on her own limited experience, she would've sketched something very close to the buildings of Triskadeka Fair.

A few times, she had the uncanny sense she'd seen a particular sight before. A blue door tugged on her memory. She swore a window box full of fading autumn blooms hung just outside somewhere back on Earth. A tarnished brass street number struck her as a thing she passed every day.

Despite feeling like she ought to remember these bits and pieces, when she focused on any detail, the familiarity vanished like steam above a cup of tea.

The commonness of the cityscape was thrown into sharp relief by the oddity of the people thronging through it. If indeed 'people' was the correct term.

An old woman bustled by. Legs exactly like a sparrow's peeked out from under the hem of her muddy black dress. Behind her, carrying her shopping bags, a half-sized man struggled to keep up. Madarena was shocked when she realized all he wore was his own extremely long grey beard, wrapped several times round his burly naked body.

"Whuh?" he gruffed, in answer to her stare.

"Come along, Ilych," the crone croaked. "You're not here to make friends."

"Not anywhere to make friends, marm."

They set to squabbling. She averted her eyes.

Please look out, a small voice spoke in her head.

She stepped to her right before realizing she was doing it. A cloud, formed into six perfectly shaped lobes, drifted by her. Flashes of multicolored light jumped from lobe to lobe as it moved.

Thank you.

The very next step, she nearly trampled a grey swarm of tiny eight-armed men and women (the spit and image of the creature who'd crawled out of the judge suit). She dodged into the street. They scuttled across the whole width of the sidewalk. They argued heatedly amongst themselves in wee piping voices. They did not notice her. They veered as one into a drab, serious building. The sign out front read: *Demosthenes, Cicero, and Grotius ATTORNEYS AT LAW.*

I wonder if they'd take my case pro bono.

Her father used the term in his practice. It meant 'working for free'. He never said it without a sarcastic twist of his lips and a roll of the eyes. For him, taking a case pro bono was like going to the dentist or visiting elderly relatives.

Madarena wasn't sure if she'd end up in Jail again or not—as Apophax, of course. If she did, she doubted magic chalk and a Plan could pay for a decent attorney.

As if summoned by thoughts of her legal troubles, an Anubis appeared round the corner. He walked in her direction, though he did not look at her. He towered over everyone in the street.

Madarena lost her head. She veered right, nearly getting run over by an enormous pink snail moving forty kilometers an hour faster than customary for gastropods. It emitted a sound like hope exploding.

On the far side of the road, she kept running. No one she shoved out of her way made a lasting impression, as disgruntled as their hue and cry was. Any minute she expected a marble hand to close on her shoulder. She pounded concrete till she couldn't go on.

She skidded to a stop.

She was lost.

Brilliant. Just stupid brilliant. Now you'll never find the Whaterry Square.

Three of the metal-and-spring Planck-people walked across the road. Two small boys skipped circles round an older woman who, Madarena presumed, was their mother.

"Excuse me!" She waved. "Hey! May I have a moment of your time?"

The mother gasped and put her hand over her mouth.

"I never!"

The boys looked away, uncomfortably. Like someone just cursed or spat something nasty on the sidewalk and was about to be punished.

"You most certainly may not, sir." She seized her boys by the hands. "The very idea!"

She led them away in a huff. She shot Madarena one last judgey look, over her shoulder. As they receded into the crowd, she lectured them on how that was a sterling example of how one ought never to behave.

Madarena's face grew hot.

How was I supposed to know?

She didn't get much of a chance to stew in embarrassment.

"Does sir see anything he would like to try on?"

A young woman floated lightly down shop steps towards her. The neat hem of her dress cut a fine line, a handspan above the dirty street. She did not have feet.

The window behind proclaimed the establishment:

Moirai Sisters Clothiers
Fates and Fashions, Bespoke
We'll Fit You
Anake

Behind the glass, dozens of fine outfits posed on mannequins of indeterminate species. Madarena had only seen such fashions in color plates of very old books, at the antiquarian bookstore she haunted during summers. Compared to the garments inside the shop, Apophax's hedgehog overcoat hung even more shabbily than before.

She was beginning to understand what her mother meant by 'disreputable'.

"If you please, this way. A change of outfit will surely soothe your turbulent spirits. Clothes make the man."

The saying was inapt in every way. Still, Madarena let herself be herded inside. The woman had a way about her that brooked no argument.

A slightly older woman sat at a table just inside the shop, marking chalk measurements on a black sack suit.

"Ah! Another discerning customer. Let's take your measure."

She rose. Like her sister, she hovered. Disconcerting.

"I'm impecunious," Madarena protested, as the shutting door shushed the Triskadeka traffic. It calmed her to use a new word the right way. She turned a couple pockets inside out to show how broke she was.

The first seamstress produced a tangled skein of thread. "We would be happy to take your old clothes in trade."

"This old thing?"

The second one unrolled a tape measure. "And we have most generous terms of credit, should you be unwilling to part with that spiny thing. For sentimental reasons."

A third woman, decades older than the others, wafted out from the back. She held a large pair of silver shears, with a thick length of leather cord between the blades.

"You will find that you have a great deal more to offer than you think you do."

Snick.

She severed the cord in a single snip. A grim shiver wriggled down Madarena's spine and out all four limbs.

"It's really ok. I should probably be going. Sorry for taking your time."

"Nonsense," said the eldest. "Clotho, dear."

The middle saleswoman blocked Madarena's path to the door. She stretched the tape measure around her various dimensions, calling out numbers. The youngest sister, whom Clotho called Lachesis, jotted down the measurements.

"I'm Atropos." The oldest Moirai snicked her scissors when she talked, an absent-minded fidget. "I didn't catch your name."

"Apophax. They call me Apophax."

"Hold still, please," Clotho said.

"I'm thinking something in obscurity," mused Lachesis.

"Obscurity. *Snick.* Or indifference? *Snick.*"

Clotho finished. "What about solitude?"

Atropos floated over to a mannequin. "No. *Snick.* Not solitude."

"Hey, I like being alone."

"Do you?" Clotho stepped back. She wound up her tape measure.

Lachesis tucked her pencil behind her ear. "Or do you just not like anyone you've ever known?"

She'd never thought about it that way. Weirdly, the sketch in Apophax's pocket popped into her mind. Aoede. Her, Madarena felt sure, she wouldn't mind hanging out with. Not that it mattered. She was a sketch. And wrapped up with Apophax, which made her suspect.

Clotho pursed her lips.

"Maybe a misanthropy duster trimmed in narcissism?"

"Don't be silly. *Snick.* We can't put her in that. *Snick.* She's much too young."

"Don't be so haughty," Lachesis butted in. "We know just as much as you."

"*Snick. Snick.*"

The sisters bickered. They drifted around the store, holding coats up and rejecting them. No one blocked the door. Fascinated by their play, Madarena forgot to escape. By the time she realized it, they'd settled on one garment each. They drifted like seaweed on warm lazy waters. She was surrounded.

Clotho held up a trench coat made of mirrored shifting silver. It reflected the Moirai, the mannequins, the passersby—everything except Madarena. She'd be nearly invisible in it.

"Isolation. Classic and contemporary, for the woman who knows she's her own best company."

Lachesis offered a taupe-on-tan cardigan so aggressively generic, Madarena's eye slid right off the ordinariness.

"Obscurity. For the child who wants to be seen and not heard. And not seen."

"Or..."

Atropos presented an ankle-length muslin hoodie. It didn't even look finished—raw cloth, frayed at the edges, the stitches all showing. It flowed nicely though.

"Potential."

"Let's try these on," Lachesis ordered. "Take off that old dream's coat, Madarena."

The sound of her real name cut through the Moirai's hypnotic spell.

She stepped back. She knocked a mannequin over. She didn't spare it a glance.

"If you know my name, you know I can't. I can't take Apophax's coat off."

"Oh?" A smirk played across Clotho's face. "Is that so?"

Lachesis whispered in her ear. "Whyever would that be?"

"Snick."

Clotho lifted up Madarena's right arm. She inspected her wrist. "It seems that someone…"

"…has stolen a length…" Lachesis lightly touched her left palm.

Atropos pointed up the sleeve. "…of Destiny Thread."

The tip of her scissors pressed into Madarena's skin. Cold. Pin-prick painful.

"All tangled up in blue," Clotho sing-songed. "What's a wicked girl to do, to do?"

Where Atropos's blade touched, a fine cerulean thread — almost too fine to be seen — circled three times round Madarena's wrist. It disappeared up the quill-lined fabric of Apophax's coat. It emerged on the other side. That thread, she could now tell, was what kept her bound in the coat. Kept her wearing Apophax's face and stuck her with his crimes.

The sisters circled her — no longer seaweed. Sharks on the prowl, waiting to frenzy.

"Can you fix it?" Madarena asked. "Like I said, I can't pay. I can work whatever off. Do you need filing done? Paperwork? I have recent legal experience!"

Snick.

"We can fix it, dear." Lachesis giggled. Not a nice giggle. "Of course we can."

"*Snick.* We can snip you right out of Apophax's coat. Send you on your way home."

Clotho made a slap-worthy smug face. "All you have to do is ask."

"What will happen to Apophax if you do that?"

"*Snick.* He won't be your problem any more."

"That's not what I asked."

"Quick now," Clotho said.

"Hurry," Lachesis hissed. "No more questions."

"Except one. *Snick.*"

"Ask our sister to cut that stolen thread," Clotho and Lachesis chanted in unison. "Untangle this mess and smooth out your story."

Madarena hovered on the edge of an awful decision.

"I need to know what will happen either way."

"You never get to know. *Snick.* Until you know. *Snick.*"

All three sisters reeled with peals of laughter at a joke whose punchline only they knew.

"NO!"

As Atropos crossed her path, Madarena shoved her hard out of the way. She snatched the unfinished hoodie. She bolted to the door. She hit the pavement running. She pounded through town till she could no longer hear the Moirai's vicious mocking taunts.

8.

Madarena dropped heavily to the edge of the sidewalk. Her heart lodged in her throat.

That's it. Even if I convince them I'm not Apophax, I'll do time for stealing.

She laid the hoodie across her lap. It wasn't a finished garment. She'd snagged a toile. At least it looked like a good fit. If she could ever get out of Apophax's quill-coat. She couldn't keep the quaver out of her voice.

"It's not even done enough to be disreputable."

Her shoulders slumped. She held her head between her hands. She stared into a dirty puddle at her feet. A pale brown reflection of that felon Apophax stared back, a worried look on his face.

"What am I supposed to do?"

She was used to trouble in little, fun ways. This was exponentially worse. She couldn't even hope to find Planck, the one person who'd been nice to her.

Pfft. Like you need anyone, a dry little voice said in the back of her head. *Isn't this what you always wanted?*

"Not like this."

So all those daydreams about living alone were just ways to waste time? Did you think you were going to live at home forever?

"It's not the same. This is real and I'm going to jail. At best. I don't even know the worst."

An iron-soled boot, crusted with dried blood, stomped the puddle dry.

"Well, well," a low, feral voice purred. "Apophax. What a coincidence. Life's a city full of straying streets, isn't it, Mistress Chironex?"

Words like skittering insects crawled over her shoulder. "It is, Master Grimsykill. Straying streets. And death's the marketplace where each one meets."

Madarena jumped to her feet.

"I'm not Apophax! Swear!"

The dry little voice, fluttering into hiding in her brain, uttered a parting shot. *Don't you get tired of saying that?*

"Of course you're not," the cruel voice mocked. "I'm sure it's all a misunderstanding."

Two nightmarish figures loomed over her. Her chest squeezed. Her vision narrowed. Her brain ordered her legs to run. Her legs seized and could not move.

The first speaker hulked, both hands on a black iron cane. His enormous humped shoulders and barrel chest had been jammed into a tweed suit several sizes too small. His eyes glowed blood-red, without irises nor whites. His face was a mottled mess of scars and bruises. He grimaced at her with all of six sharp teeth.

"A misunderstanding, he says."

Beside him crouched a huge insectoid shape, wrapped entirely within a poison-green silk robe. Her voice crawled cross Madarena's skin like roaches. "Misunderstandings seem to follow Apophax everywhere, don't they?"

Had she straightened up, she would've been a giant. She hunched doubled over, like a mantis. A deep cowled hood hid her face. Too many eyes glittered from inside its folds. She held her arms crooked in front of her. Instead of hands, two chitonous scythes, thin and sharp as razors, twitched just under the edges of her trumpet sleeves.

It took all the strength Madarena had to fake some confidence instead of screaming.

"Oh, good! So you know him. A complete rat, right?"

She forced one foot forward with a casual step.

"I'll just be on my way. Good luck—"

THWAP!

Grimsykill's cane hit her chest. Not hard enough to hurt much. Just hard enough to let her know how much more it *could* hurt if he wanted.

"Here's the thing."

"Yes," Chironex chittered. "The thing."

"The Night Mayor's offered a great deal for your demise."

"And even more if he gets to watch," Chironex said.

The Night Mayor? From the plan! the incongruous thought came, oblivious to the danger.

Grimsykill clucked. "We're not greedy though, Mistress."

Chironex's scythe-like forearms clicked. A similar click came from within her hood.

"What's that?" Grimsykill said. "Oh. It seems I was mistaken, Apophax. We *are* greedy."

"S-so what you're saying is th-there's room to n-negotiate?"

Madarena wished ever so hard she hadn't stuttered.

"I can pay —"

"I AM TALKING!" Grimsykill roared. The head of his cane struck sparks from the sidewalk.

"Best listen," Chironex whispered into the dead silence that followed.

"You've gone too far. Stealing Aoede? Bad. Losing her to the Logons? So much worse. I don't recall if there are any of his many, many, *many* possessions that the Night Mayor is fonder of than the damsel. Do you, Mistress?"

"None. So fond. He loves that statue."

Statue?

Madarena was keenly aware of the lump in her slipper, where she'd hid the Plan with the breathtaking drawing on the flip side of the page.

Grimsykill buffed the head of his cane on one tight-stretched lapel. "So you see, you really did earn this killing we're going to give you."

"Back in Oneiros."

Grimsykill bristled with impatience. "Yes, yes, Mistress. In Oneiros. In front of the Night Mayor. For the extra bounty."

He waved one paw at Madarena. "You may make noise now."

She backed into Chironex. The assassin felt crunchy under her silks. Madarena shuddered. No Anubis in sight. In fact, the street was completely deserted. It was just her.

She dug deep and found anger and cunning beneath her terror.

"Alright. You want noise? I'll make—"

Mid-sentence, she hurled herself at Grimsykill's chest. Last minute, she tucked her shoulder and hit him square in the belly. He cried out as the spines of the overcoat pierced his skin. His suit, already strained beyond reason, split at the punctures. Great rips shot up and down, revealing more angry red scars.

"DIE!" he roared.

One huge paw grabbed her. When it closed on her back, the coat-quills stabbed him again. He dropped his cane and wrung his hand, cursing.

Madarena stepped on the cane's head. The sharp tip flipped up. She caught the stick in the middle. She spun about face.

Chironex lashed down with both bladed arms. Madarena ducked. She stuck the iron bar out, catching the razors crosswise. Chironex's claws sunk into the cane. They did not cut all the way through. She pulled it out of Madarena's hand. She struggled to free herself.

Madarena rolled to one side, away from the bellowing thug and hissing assassin. She tumbled end over end. She regained her feet. She sprinted down the block.

At the corner, she spared a glance back. Grimsykill extricated his cane from Chironex's claws with a great yank. They loped up the street towards her.

Pell-mell once more she fled through Triskadeka Fair. She dove into a crowd, hoping to elude her pursuers. They proved relentless. Every time she looked back, there they were.

At long last, she found herself trapped. Looking up at the three steep walls that penned her in a dead-end alley, she had only one regret. She would never get her hands round Apophax's scrawny neck.

Even for just a second, she fiercely thought, *to wring the wicked out of him.*

The click of Chironex's razor claws and the tap of Grimsykill's cane grew closer and closer. Too close for her to get away. Fear banished fantasies of revenge.

She cast around for something to help. The alley's only features were a line of drying laundry, a wash bucket full of sudsy water, and the faded chalk outline of an old hopscotch game.

"CHALK!"

She snapped her fingers. She fished out the magic chalk.

Hastened by the impending *tap-tap-tap* and *click-click-click* she tore a bedsheet off the line. She drew a wide squobbly circle on the pavement, about a meter in front of the wash bucket. Using the last of the chalk, she shaded in the edges, to provide the illusion of depth. She spread the sheet over the drawing of the deep pit.

Six seconds later, the killers appeared at the alley's mouth.

"It was just business," Grimsykill snarled. "You went and made it personal."

They rushed her.

As they crossed the sheet, they plunged into the pit. They scrabbled at the sheet, trying to pull themselves back up. It slid down over the cobbles too quickly. In an instant, they were gone. Foul words roared up from the hole.

"Feh. Such language."

She kicked over the wash bucket. A wave of dirty, soapy water washed over the chalk drawing. She snatched a towel. She scrubbed out the sketch with all her might.

"HA!" she crowed to the assassins' dwindling howls.

Having erased the hole, she stepped back. The wet towel dropped with a satisfying *splurtch.* Only the iron cane, still rolling on the pavement, remained of Grimsykill and Chironex.

"Woot!"

She snatched up the stick. She twirled it. She danced a flailing victory jig.

"Not entirely unimpressive," a wry voice said from high above.

Madarena stopped dead in her dance.

She knew that voice.

"I'm not sure I could've done it better," Apophax continued. "I applaud your quick thinking."

Perched high atop the wall, spindly legs dangling down, the pot-bellied rogue gave her a dainty hand clap.

Hard as she could, she hurled the cane straight at his head.

9.

A cane, however useful it might be for drubbing someone about the head and shoulders, makes an unwieldy thrown weapon. This is doubly true if one is (as Madarena was) blind with rage.

Grimsykill's stick flew end over end to a spot on the wall well below Apophax's dangling feet. The clenched lead fist hit with a BAM! A chunk of brick flew across the alley. The cane clattered to the ground.

"I see you're one of those people who can't take a compliment."

Nimbly for a man his age, he scampered down the wall. Madarena lunged for the cane. Too quick for her, he seized it.

"It takes practice," he continued, holding the truncheon out of her reach. "Next time, try a simple curtsy and humble 'Oh, a mere bagatelle'."

Unable to get the cane, Madarena (who ordinarily was not at all violent) stomped hard on the old man's foot.

"OW!" he cried in a most satisfying fashion.

"Oh," she curtsied. "A mere bagatelle."

Then she (who truly almost never resorted to this kind of savagery) kicked him hard in the shin. He hopped around, waving his hands in submission.

"Peace! Peace!"

She calmly bent down for the sopping towel. "Peace?"

She twirled it till it was a nice, tight rat-tail.

"Peace?!"

She snapped his backside with a loud POP!

"PEACE YOU SAY?!"

She surprised herself with the vehemence of her violence. It felt so good to visit a portion of her recent misfortunes on their source. She chased Apophax around the alley, popping him with the towel. His pained yelps abated her rage somewhat. By the time he cowered in the corner, she felt more like her usual dulcet, forgiving self.

Her arm was also tired.

She dropped the wet towel on his head. He whimpered pitifully.

"Oh hush. Serves you right. Do you have any idea how much trouble you've stuck me with?"

He sniffled. "Probably less than I would have been in, if it had been me instead of you."

"You!" She drew back one foot. He quailed under her strong tone.

Angry as she was, Madarena wasn't the sort of hard person who could kick an old man while he was down, no matter how wicked he was. She waited for the red spots to clear from her eyes. She picked up the cane. She prodded him.

"Up you go. Come on."

He kipped up. The signs of distress vanished.

"Now that you've got that out of your system," he brushed his hands clean, "let's talk about settling our accounts."

She couldn't believe she'd fallen for his act. Again. She considered whacking him with the cane. Sadly, her moment of madness had passed and she didn't have another whipping in her.

"One," he ticked items off on his long clever fingers, "you used up the last of my Ontochalk. Don't know when I'll get back to Ontos and, judging from the length and volume of pursuit as I left, it was very, very expensive."

"Send me a bill."

"Don't think I won't."

"You know where I live."

"Two. It looks as though you've stolen a hoodie from the Moirai. They'll add that to my tab, the reckoning of which is becoming untenably dear."

"I tried selling them your coat. They wanted to cut the Destiny Thread."

Apophax's face blanched. "Hrm. Rmph. Gruffle. You didn't let them, obviously. A wise choice. I'll spot you the hoodie as a reward."

"Are you sure? We can go back and I can explain. Atropos seemed really into her scissors."

He pointedly ignored her. "Three. There's the obvious matter, as yet unbroached, of your escape from Triskadeka Jail. That adds the charge of flight from justice to the long list of ridiculous invented crimes the Logons think I've committed."

"Invented?"

"All crimes are invented, if you think about it."

"You are terrible."

"Insulting your benefactor. You truly are a savage adolescent. Who mannered you? If this is your typical behavior, I don't see why I should waste my benevolence on you."

Madarena goggled. She could not believe his nerve. "Benef—? Sava—? Mann—?"

A dozen objections to his gall rushed to her mouth. They all crammed in together, stuck. All she could manage was a spibbling noise.

"I am a fair man," he continued. "I'm willing to prorate the use of the chalk, rather than expecting you to recompense me for a whole stick."

The spibbling turned into a *fruh fruh fruh.*

"And I do suppose you can be forgiven for not adequately defending me at trial. You did your best and that clearly isn't very good."

Madarena emitted a shallow whuffing, interspersed with deep growls.

"I tell you what. I'll relieve you of this troublesome truncheon," he tugged Grimsykill's cane from her stunned lax grip. "And I'll take back this sartorial artifact I so kindly leant you."

With a flick of his wrist, the quill-coat flapped off Madarena's back, like a magician's tablecloth from under a stack of dinner plates.

CRACK!

The pavement at her feet broke open a hair. With a grinding sound, the fissure widened.

"Assuming," Apophax said, bunching up for a sprint, "you are as attached to your continued existence as I am to mine, I would suggest—"

That's as far as he got before she was out of earshot.

"Good idea," he panted, catching up to her several blocks away. "Maybe more of a brisk walk. Fit in. Less attention from the Anubises."

She saw the wisdom in it.

"And put your hoodie on. You're still wearing your nightgown and robe."

Without breaking stride, she shrugged it on. She wrapped it tightly around herself. She thought the most innocent thoughts she could. In no time at all, she and Apophax were in a city park, well-mingled with the crowd, with nary a sign of Grimsykill or Chironex.

"You're a natural at this."

Her pleasure at the compliment annoyed her. Why did she care if he thought she was good at something? Best be quit with him for good.

"We should split up."

"Quite. Prior to your egress, stage left, hold still for a bit of chicanery."

"What?"

He plucked a quill from the edge of his coat. "It works best if you don't move."

"What does? What are you doing?"

"Sowing chaos."

He bent down to her shadow, stretched long on the white snow that covered the lawn. He scratched the sharp quill-tip around the entire inside of the dark patch, creating a thin outline. He peeled away a line of black.

"The trick is in the wrist. Always in the wrist."

He looped the excised strand around his fingers, like a cat's cradle. He puffed on the black threads. They inflated until they merged into a copy of her shadow.

"This is the hard bit."

He shook out the flat shade like a wet dress. It billowed. It swelled to three dimensions. It filled with color.

Madarena stared back at a blank of herself.

"You're a fearful girl," Apophax whispered in the Shadowrena's ear. "You're going to run away from Grimsykill and Chironex. If you see them, you will shout for the nearest Anubis, wailing and carrying on in terror."

The shadow's eyes widened. Her chest heaved. Her head swiveled every which way. She yelped once and tore off across the park.

"That should confuse matters somewhat."

She hated to admit it. That had impressed her.

"What *are* you?"

Apophax buffed his fingernails on his lapel. "One doesn't like to brag. I'm just a simple dream with a few meagre talents at his disposal."

She thought about Planck's inexplicable devotion to the old grifter. Maybe there was more to him than scams and cons. She shook her head.

Don't get suckered.

"Alright. Split up. I'm out."

"For the best. I've got to see a man about a watch. And as for you, I don't want to know what shenanigans you're up to, young woman. You're entirely too unsavory a character for a gentleman of my rectitude."

"Feh."

That was when Madarena neglected to mention the Plan, wadded up under her foot. She decided to keep it. Apophax's bloviating aside, *he* owed *her* and not the other way round. The Plan and the inconvenience of its loss would be how she'd collect on the debt.

With that, they parted ways.

10.

As luck would have it, the park had a map of the city's main features. Madarena was able to locate Orrery Square and make her way there with no further trouble.

"Imprecation!" she couldn't help cry as she rounded the last corner.

The Orrery was glorious. Twice as big as her parents' house, it consisted of thirteen nested gleaming brass hoops, each as thick as her waist. The hoops floated, unsupported by any visible cables, a hundred meters above the Square. Every hoop canted at a different angle, so no two lay on the same plane.

Triskadekans—Madarena had decided that was her catch-all term for the bewildering array of species who populated the town—walked to and fro around the spectacle. Most did not spare it a glance.

A single ebony sphere nested along each hoop's length. Because of these globes, she could tell that the hoops turned, very slowly. At the center of the enormous contraption, a glowing white globe hung in a half-shell of purest silver. This mirror reflected the light in a wide beam across the turning hoops.

The light beam had almost traversed a sphere labeled COSMOS. As the Orrery rotated, the beam would soon touch a different orb. That one, like all the others save COSMOS, did not have an illuminated name.

A cone of light shone from the COSMOS sphere. It cast a wide circle of light on the stone floor of the plaza. Several kiosks stood in a line just outside the light. A labyrinth of red velvet ropes surrounded the whole thing. It reminded Madarena of an airport security line. No one waited in the rope maze. Only one kiosk was occupied. At that distance she could not see much detail of the functionary who tended it.

Not that it matters. Shouldn't go tangling with anyone official anyway.

She scanned the crowd. Planck hadn't arrived. She found a bench off to the side. She marveled a while at the Orrery. What did it all mean? Thirteen? There were only eight planets and none of them was named Cosmos. The hypnotic megasculpture crept round in its languorous pace.

She woolgathered. Her mind drifted this way and that. Her gaze softened. Each blink lengthened. It took effort to hold her chin off her chest.

She had, after all, been up all night.

With a jolt, she tumbled from the bench. Limbs akimbo, she flailed to the ground. The hard marble of the piazza bruised her elbow and knee. A sudden flood of adrenaline yanked her from the hypnogogic fuzz between sleep and wake.

"Impr—" She checked herself. No sense in wasting an imprecation. "Get up, woman. Sleeping on a bench? That's some Apophaxian shenanigans right there. Dis-incredibly-reputable."

She spoke loudly, to keep the flutters of slumber away. She plonked her haunches back on the bench hard. She stiffened her spine.

And in no time at all, the cotton folds of drowsiness stuffed in from the corners of her eyes. The nodding-off began again.

"BLEH!"

She stood up. She shook out her arms and legs. She paced back and forth in front of the bench.

"Seriously? You can't fall asleep when you want to and you can't stay awake when you want to? Make up your mind, hypothalamus!"

She pictured the little peanut-sized piece of her brain responsible for telling the rest of it when to sleep and when to wake. She wished she could jab it into compliance. Or at least get the other grey matter to slap it around a little.

She needed a distraction. The Orrery swung like a mesmerist's glitter bob.

The lump in her slipper proved the key. She retrieved the Plan. Now that she knew a little more about Apophax et al., she might be able to suss out more details from the cryptic diagram.

At least it would be a problem to solve. Otherwise she'd nod off. Who knew where she'd wake up?

If she'd wake up.

She unfolded the Plan on the bench. She started at the beginning.

This Night Mayor person, whoever he was, was the main mark of Apophax's con. He was also, if Grimsykill and Chironex were any indication, a villain himself. She couldn't fault Apophax for stealing from someone who kept those two on the payroll.

Oddly, she didn't see the assassins anywhere in the Plan. Either Apophax hadn't expected them or he didn't think they were important enough to include. Neither made sense, given her brief interaction with them. She shuddered at the memory.

Tracing the connections, she realized that Aoede—the 'damsel' statue who was the target of the heist—had been stored somewhere called The City of Dreams. She studied over the various names and ploys Apophax had used to pilfer her from the Night Mayor's vaults.

The term 'quid pro quo' came up a lot.

She recognized it as another legal term her father liked to throw around. It meant 'this for that'. For instance, if she asked him to buy her a book at the antiquarian store, he'd say 'quid pro quo' and she'd have to figure out what kind of chore ('quo') would convince him to get it ('quid').

Much practice had made her good at that game. Very, very good.

The answer usually involved the most boring task humankind had ever created. Filing paperwork in an office. If she'd ever needed to prove her love of dusty old books to a judge, the ennui-filled hours squandered on organizing tedious briefs would've been more than sufficient evidence.

"So you play 'quid pro quo' too," she murmured to the absent scoundrel. "You as good as me?"

The Plan piqued her interest. An itchy part of her brain wished she had met Apophax under better circumstances. She could have learned a lot from the old man.

Shut up.

You know it's true.

"Excuse me?"

A tin finger tapped on her arm. She snapped out of her reverie.

"Planck! You made it!"

"On time and not a minute past." His bright eyes drifted across the wide unfolded paper beside her. "Is that what I think it is?"

Unconsciously, she shifted to cover the Plan.

"Yes. You haven't seen it before?"

"No. I didn't ask any questions. Hearing your story, though, I wish I had."

"I'm sure it's—hold on! How did you know it was me? The last time you saw me I was all old and crufty on account of the coat."

"That was confusing, yes. Now, your time's still the same as it was and it looks like it matches you. I mean, the same as time ever is. It's changing the same ways, all the ways out."

"That makes no sense."

He slapped his forehead with a metallic *tink!* "Of course! Sorry. I haven't met very many non-Chronons."

"Chronon. Oneiron," she said, thinking aloud. She re-read the name on the illuminated sphere. "Cosmon?"

"Yes! That's what you are. At least, judging by the time you arrived in Triskadeka Fair. And Apophax is an Oneiron and I'm a Chronon. We can see your time, the same way you see off into the distance. Like if you look across the Square. See the other side?"

"There's people in the way, but sure, mostly."

"That's how seeing your time is. I can't tell you to the second how far you have any more than you can tell me to the centimeter how far away the other side of the Square is. I can get a general idea. There's optical illusions too. Like that coat—I couldn't figure out if you were old or young. You flipped between the two."

"What did Apophax offer you? And what were you going to do for him? Was it just the jail break?"

Planck's face fell at the sudden blunt questions.

"Sorry. It's just—you're very nice and you seem pretty honest and even if I don't understand it all, there's a lot of shenanigans."

He looked at his feet. "I know. I mean, I know now. I didn't know then."

"How could you not? If you can see through time—"

"—it's not perfect!"

His vehemence startled her. She'd upset him. She hadn't wanted to and now she'd angered the one friend she had in this meshuga place. For the first time in her life, she wished she were better with people.

"I'm sorry. We don't have to talk about it."

He replied quietly. "It's not your fault. I'm just mad at myself for being tricked."

"I can relate. Let's be mad at Apophax instead."

Planck smiled. "I'd prefer to be mad at no one. Talk about a waste of time!"

Just like that, his chipper demeanor returned. She really had never met anyone so nice.

"So you wanted to know what he offered me?" he said. "Adventure!"

"Adventure?"

"I wanted adventure, excitement, the chance to be something more than a petty time-server in a big coggy machine, spending my life redeeming other people's time."

Madarena remembered all the times her father had talked about 'billable hours'. It had sounded ghastly. She got how Planck felt.

"Along came Apophax and says, 'Two things, Planck m'boy, and I'll spring you from the cuckoo clock for good.'"

"Feh."

"The things he showed me though. Oh, Madarena! Dreams are tricky and beautiful!"

"So he wanted you to pick him up outside the Triskadeka Jail. Which meant he had an escape route already planned."

She wondered if it was the same ploy she'd come up with. In that case, him complaining about her using up his chalk was even more egregious.

"To the minute, remarkably. That's what I meant when I said 'great' wasn't a good enough word for him. He makes clever look slow as hot summer seconds when you're waiting for a cool fall breeze."

"I reiterate: 'feh'."

"The second thing was this."

Planck held out his hand. He dangled a tarnished bronze timepiece on a cheap copper chain. It did not tick.

"A broken stopwatch?" She did not recall seeing that in the Plan.

"Thirty-seven seconds. Even Pruftock's been-counters aren't so persnickety. They round losses to the nearest minute."

He dropped the watch. Reflexively, Madarena caught it.

"And there you go. You can give that to Apophax when you see him."

"I'm done with him."

"Maybe. Maybe not. He has a way of tangling people up."

That was the same word the Moirai had used. Made her wrist itch just thinking about it.

"No. Here. Take it. You give it to him. He won't quo you unless you quid him."

Planck shook his head.

"I'm done with that. It was fun to imagine a life of adventure. When I heard your story though... and then I stole thirty-seven seconds!"

His hands wrung. Madarena patted him on the arm to comfort him. It did not work.

"My gears got all grindy, deep inside. My whole body felt like a pendulum that was swinging faster and faster until it would fly off into space and never stop!"

"That sounds exciting, not bad."

"That's the difference between you and me. That's why I'm going back to my job. Better to imagine what might be and plod a steady pace than take another tick of this jangling craziness."

"Hold on. Here, look!"

She flipped the Plan over to reveal the drawing of Aoede. Even with the clatter of the Orrery and the chatter of the crowd, the distant mystical music arose in her mind. From the way Planck swayed in rhythm, she could tell he heard it too.

"Ticks and tocks..." he whispered. "She's timeless."

"She's what Apophax is trying to steal. I don't know why he needed you for that. Not yet. But he did need you and so you *have* to come along. So we can mess up his plan and keep him from getting Aoede. She needs... she needs..."

Madarena trailed off. She realized she did not know what the woman in the strange vivid drawing needed. All she knew was she would do anything she could to make sure it happened.

Planck hesitated. His face wrestled in awful agony.

"I'm sorry," he said at last. "I can't. I just can't. She's remarkable, I know. It's just that even the first steps of helping Apophax threw me so out of order I don't know how I'll get wound properly back. I can't take another tick."

"I understand," she said, though really she did not. With a regretful good-bye, Planck left her there, lost in thought.

11.

She couldn't argue with Planck's decision. Everyone had to make their own choices, she knew.

It was not, however, who she could ever be. Angry as she'd been at Apophax, when she read his Plan, she automatically latched onto it. Her brain kicked into overdrive trying to figure it out—and plot out how to make it better.

She liked shenanigans.

Her world till that point had been too small. She'd dreamt of adventure. And, unlike Planck, she'd taken every chance life had given her to stir things up and make things more interesting.

Where does that leave you? she asked herself.

She had no answer.

She put the watch away. Wistfully brushing Aoede's sketch with her fingertips, she folded the plan back up. She stuffed the paper wad back in her slipper. She stood up. She put resolute hands on her hips, in the hopes that would inspire action.

It did not.

Overhead, the COSMOS sphere clicked nigh-imperceptibly on its course out of the beam of light.

Ok. Planck said you were a Cosmon. That means from Cosmos. From the Greek word for 'the universe'.

Apparently, the sardonic side of her interjected, *the universe isn't all there is. Don't tell scientists. They'll have to reprint everything.*

Shush.

She meandered 'round the Square, eyes fixed on the Orrery.

Those stairs to the Judge were made of the same kind of light. That looks like an airport security line. Therefore, I can at least get back to my reality if I go there.

The cosmos, Sardonic Madarena helpfully offered, *is a really big place.*

Do you have a better idea? No, you do not. You never do.

Like a rat in a maze, she navigated the roped-off part of the Square. Even if the beam dropped her off far from home, she felt confident she could manage. In fact, the idea excited her. Her parents would be simultaneously baffled and furious when she popped up on another continent.

At the end of the queue, a uniformed mannequin sat behind a kiosk.

"Passport?" it asked in a tinny voice.

Logon.

A frisson prickled her forearms. Somewhere inside the Security Guard lurked a tiny, officious bug.

"Beg pardon?" she asked, to buy herself a second to think.

"Passport."

The only passport she had to offer was Apophax's. She could measure to the nanometer exactly how bad an idea that would be.

"Here's the thing. I lost my passport earlier today. Not sure where it is. It might be stolen. Probably by someone named Apophax—I'm positive it was him, now that I think about it. Short, bald, totally disreputable?"

"Name?"

"Madarena Rua. M, A, D..."

A faint tapping echoed inside the Security Guard Shell.

"Date of entry?"

"Yesterday."

More tapping. A ominous bureaucratic pause. Faster tapping. A longer, and hence even more ominous pause. Very slow tapping. A pause so long, Madarena almost lost track of the ominousity.

"There seems to be an issue."

Madarena didn't need to get all the way to the ISSs in her dictionary to know when a Logon said 'issue' they meant 'very bad thing for you.'

"Oh. Never mind then. Guess I'll extend my stay."

She backed away, trying not to look like she was backing away.

"It's fine, I'll just maybe, I dunno, take in some more sights, maybe find some lunch. Where's good round here? Any recommendations? Lunch, lunch, lunch."

Her left heel hit hard marble. She reached back. She patted.

"Please come with me to the Strandhome until your parent or legal guardian can collect you."

"Imprecation."

12.

A grey building hulked at the end of a cul-de-sac. A half-dozen black gables crowned its dilapidated bulk. A scrabbly excuse for a garden surrounded it with thorns. The Anubis prodded her towards a drab door with flaking paint. The sign over the door read STRANDHOME.

A Dickensian workhouse. Great.

She did not move. The Anubis reached over her. He pressed the doorbell.

A whiff of dust and dead lavender drifted out of the opening door. Madarena sneezed three times.

A woman in a high-necked charcoal dress sporting an enormous bustle stepped down to street level. Her iron-grey hair was pulled back into a bun so severe, Madarena wondered how she could move her face. Then she noticed the severe expression never changed.

"Welcome, new Strandling," a tinny voice piped from within. "Thank you, Anubis, that is all."

"I will wait until she is inside. She is a runner."

"Is she?" The Logon's disapproval radiated through the suit. "Duly noted."

She stiffly nodded.

"I am the Headmistress. You may call me Headmistress. There is no need for the definite article, unless that is customary in your native locality."

"Pleased to meet you." Madarena threw in an ironic curtsy. "You may call me The Madarena. I am the definite article."

"How... individual." Her tone—exactly like Madarena's mother's saying the exact same word—made it crystal clear how low her opinion was of that particular adjective.

On her way inside, Madarena scanned the windows. They were all barred, boarded, or shuttered. Bars might be a problem. Boards and shutters, she could pry off, given enough time.

Something told her she would have plenty of time.

The door shut with a sepulchral thud.

"You should know, The Madarena, I will not brook insolence. Also forbidden are recalcitrance and obstreperousness."

Madarena repeated the words.

"Have you got a dictionary?"

Headmistress raised a hand. Before she could strike, the doorbell rang again. Madarena's heart jumped in her chest. She hoped it was Planck, there to rescue her.

Headmistress extended a knobby finger towards the wall. It was covered in the dullest, greyest wallpaper Madarena had ever seen.

"Stand there and wait. Chin up, eyes forward, back straight."

With a confident swagger, Madarena complied. It had to be Planck. She knew the sweet tick-tock boy would come to his senses.

When Headmistress opened the door, two corpses, decayed and staring with liquid white eyes, waited on the stoop.

"GAH!"

"Silence!" Headmistress snapped.

Then, unctuously to the zombies: "Terribly sorry. The Madarena is a new Strandling and not yet aware of all of our rules. Do come in, Mr. and Mrs. Rotwell."

The undead couple shambled in. They smelled terrible, and it took all of Madarena's discipline not to pull her robe up over her nose and mouth. She could only tell them apart because Mr. Rotwell wore a pair of cargo shorts and knee-length black socks, while his wife wore a tattered executive power suit. He must have been on vacation while she worked.

"Duhhhhzhheeee..." he groaned.

"Yes, of course," Headmistress said. "Your daughter has been here since the Stair passed out of alignment with Thanatos last year. I will have her fetched at once."

She stepped on a button on the floor, just beside the base of a flight of stairs leading up. Madarena heard a distant tinkle. Her fear began to subside. If Headmistress treated zombies in the foyer as a matter of course, it must be fine.

"Was your walk up pleasant?" Headmistress asked.

"Whurrr," said Mrs. Rotwell.

"Mrruuhhhh," said Mr. Rotwell, nodding his head.

Mrs. Rotwell smiled. A fat maggot crawled out the gap in her yellow teeth. It fell to the grey carpet. "Fruhhhh fruhhhh," she said.

"Oh, indeed," said Headmistress, snatching an umbrella from a stand by the door and discreetly skewering the grub on the tip. "The first few steps are always so delightful. One does like to look back and see things so small."

"Smurrrr," agreed Mr. Rotwell, in a tone of blank sagacity.

The wall next to Madarena opened. Another shell-person emerged — a short, stocky man with a round face that, had it been any shade of color but grey, would have been pleasant.

"Yes, Headmistress?"

"Beadle, please fetch Daisy Rotwell from the Workroom."

"Yes ma'am," Beadle said. He disappeared back into the wall.

Everyone stood awkwardly around the foyer, in the way grown-ups do when they're waiting without much more to say.

"Are you here for business or pleasure?" Headmistress asked after a while.

At the same time, however, Mr. Rotwell bent down to Madarena. "Thruuhhh ruhhmmm tuhhh?" he asked. His breath was atrocious. Madarena did not trust herself to answer without throwing up.

"The Madarena just arrived from Cosmos yesterday," Headmistress answered.

To Madarena's relief, Mr. Rotwell stood back up. "Kuhhh? Lurrrrrmmm, urrrr thrurrr."

"It *is* lovely this time of year," Madarena said, irritation overcoming the last bits of fear.

She *hated* people talking over her the way Headmistress had. "Though cold, of course."

She had no idea what the zombie was saying. She guessed it was probably the dull things adults say to fill up space. She knew how to play that game, even with the walking dead.

"Bruhh!" exclaimed Mrs. Rotwell, evidently able to relate.

"And where do you come from?"

"The Rotwells," Headmistress said, sternly regaining control of the conversation, "are from Thanatos. As you obviously know."

Madarena glared at her. Placidly oblivious, Headmistress made some trivial observation about the shopping in Triskadeka Fair.

She was interrupted by Beadle's re-appearance, accompanying Daisy Rotwell. She was a zombie-girl about Madarena's age. She wore a frock and smock that were exactly the same shade of grey as the wallpaper and carpet. One eye looked left and the other right. Most disconcertingly (to Madarena, at least), she had no lower jaw at all.

"Huhnff hunfff," she said.

"Dhuhhthuhh yuhhr juh," Mrs. Rotwell said. Somehow, Madarena knew Daisy was in trouble. She caught her left-looking eye and winked in solidarity.

The other girl sneered. She rolled her one rollable eye.

Sheesh. Even the dead have mean girls.

Mrs. Rotwell pulled a jawbone out of her purse. Daisy shuffled forward. She reached for it. Instead of letting her put it back, though, her mother held the back of her head and pushed the bone into place herself.

"Muhhhtherrrr," Daisy said. "Puhhhleeasse."

She worked the jaw up and down, embarrassed. Her mother stuffed a booklet in her hand. It reminded Madarena of Apophax's passport.

"Hrrrd on isshhh tiii."

"Muhhh!"

Amazing, Madarena thought, how maternal condescension transcended mortality.

Mr. Rotwell took out his wallet. A clot of black dirt fell out as well, crumbling all over the carpet. "Mruhhh?"

"No charge at all," Headmistress said. "We are funded by the Strandling Labor Initiative."

"Thurrrr?"

"Quite sure. As a duly appointed Warden of Triskadeka Fair, I couldn't accept personal remuneration. Rest in peace, the SLI stipend is most sufficient."

"Mruh." Contented, Mr. Rotwell, putting his wallet away.

Mrs. Rotwell grabbed Daisy's upper arm firmly. Her fingers sunk into the zombie flesh. Her mother groaned at her ceaselessly as they left. Daisy grunted back from time to time. Madarena felt bad for the girl—she probably hadn't *meant* to get stuck in Triskadeka Fair.

After the Rotwells were gone, Headmistress locked two deadbolts and a key lock on the front door, *thunk* after *thunk* after ominous *thunk*. She scraped the maggot off the tip of the umbrella onto the carpet. It left a wet streak in the dirt that had fallen from Mr. Rotwell's pocket.

"Beadle, I must attend to the completion of the Rotwells' paperwork. Please set The Madarena to what is left of Daisy's daily tasks. And tell Maid that we have quite a mess in the foyer."

"Yes, ma'am."

With that, the Suit swept stiffly out of sight.

"Please follow me," Beadle said. He went down the hall, past the stairs.

With a longing glance at the locked front door, Madarena complied. "May I ask questions now?"

"There is, to my knowing, no rule against asking a Beadle questions."

"A Beadle?" Madarena asked, catching the indefinite article. "Are there more than one of you?"

"Beadle is a position. For now, it is mine."

"Are you one of those spider-creatures too? And Headmistress?"

"I am a Logon, yes. As is Headmistress."

"Logon," Madarena said. She mulled the word in her mind. "From Logos?"

"Yes."

"So, if Chronons like Planck are all about time and Thanatons like the Rotwells are all about gross zombies, what are you Logons all about?"

"I believe you've misunderstood what Thanatons are, as you put it, 'all about.'"

Beadle opened a door at the end of the hall. A circular staircase went up and down just beyond.

"Up this way."

Madarena did not follow up on the Thanatons. She found herself rather leery of knowing more about them.

"So? Logons?" she pressed instead.

Beadle's answer sounded like something her father might have rattled off by rote. It was delivered without inflection.

"Logos is the source of all the laws, bylaws, rules, regulations, decrees, statutes, mandates, and other dictated behaviors, whether imperative, optional but encouraged, or merely customary but perforce binding through long usage."

He opened a door on the second floor. "This way."

Madarena went through first.

"On the other hand," Beadle continued, passing her to lead down another grey hall, "that particular definition is the subject of some debate."

"Oh naturally. There would be debate."

"There are those," Beadle continued, "who hold that Logos is the repository of all the laws, bylaws, rules, regulations, decrees, statutes, mandates, and other dictated behaviors, whether imperative, optional but encouraged, or merely customary but perforce binding through long usage."

"I can see why that would be an issue."

"Oh yes!" Beadle completely missed her sarcasm.

"One imagines some vehement back and forth on the subject."

"Not merely back and forth. There are numerous contentious variants between those two positions."

"Do tell!"

"For instance, a significant faction of Logons have recently taken to arguing, if you can believe such a thing, that Logos is the *source* of all the laws, bylaws, rules, regulations, and decrees, while being the *repository* of all the statutes, mandates, and other dictated behaviors, whether imperative, optional but encouraged, or merely customary but perforce binding through long usage."

"They're mad!" Madarena fluttered a delicate hand to her chest.

"If you think that's mad, you should hear about the Inscriptionalists," Beadle said. "But that's for another time. Here is the workroom."

Ugh. Smells like corpses and boredom.

A single dim lamp hung from the ceiling in the center of the room. The large windows would have let in bright streaming day had they not been shuttered tight.

Yes!

Madarena mentally fist-pumped at the good luck to be in a room with boarded windows instead of bars. She began searching the room for something to use as a prybar.

A long metal table occupied the middle of the office. At one end rose a tall, neat stack of grey paper. Next to it were seven significantly smaller stacks, of varying heights, of identical grey sheaves.

"Oh no. Paperwork."

"I see you're familiar with the concept. Good."

She smiled. If Beadle had an ounce of human sense, he would've taken a step back from that smile. Instead, he indicated the tall stack of paper at the left end of the table.

"This is the unsorted pile. Sort them by color. Daisy has already begun the process, so you have only to follow along."

The piles were all grey. So was every sheet in the tall stack.

"By color?"

"I apologize. Headmistress did not explain you are slow. I will provide any additional explanation of the task you require."

Madarena restrained herself with great effort. "Please. Do."

It was a wonder the whole house didn't hear her teeth grinding.

"I will show you the first few, to help you get started."

He took the topmost sheet of paper from the tall stack. He placed it on one of the smaller stacks.

"See? Thusly. By color."

He took the next sheet and placed it on a different stack.

"They are organized by color," he repeated, as if she were a toddler. "Now you try one."

Madarena pinched the next grey piece of paper. She held it up to the feeble lamplight. She compared it to each pile, one at a time. She squinted till her eyes watered. She thought she just *might* see a slight difference in shade of grey between the seven piles. She dropped the piece of paper on the one in the middle.

"No. By color." Beadle's tone never changed. Like he was being very patient with someone very stupid.

He moved the sheet one to the left. "Try again."

After four tries, she managed to match the right shade of grey from the tall pile with the right shade of grey on the sorted pile. Statistically, it would have been difficult for her not to eventually get it right.

"Good job," Beadle said. He patted her on the head. "Please consider that your contractually entitled compliment for learning a simple task."

He opened the door, being sure to block the exit with his whole body.

"I will return in an hour with the next stack to be sorted."

When he closed the door behind him, Madarena strained her ears. Hope flared in her heart when she did not hear him lock it. The dull click of a key and thunk of a bolt snuffed that out like a candle wick.

13.

She didn't wallow. With Beadle gone, she could ransack the room.

No luck. Short of taking apart the metal table and using one of its broken legs, she was bereft of prybar-like objects.

That would be vandalism.

Oh well.

She bent at the knees (as one always should when lifting something heavy) and strained.

The table did not budge.

It had been bolted to the floor.

Smart.

She turned her attention to the shutters. She wriggled her fingers between the bottom board and the sill. She tugged till her fingertips screamed. It refused to move. Both shutters had been nailed to the frame all around the perimeter.

Double smart.

Her belly growled.

I wonder if they serve gruel. Like Oliver Twist. 'Please, sir' –

Shut. Up.

"Why didn't I keep that cane?" she muttered.

Because Apophax got it first.

Feh. Him.

She collapsed cross-legged to the floor. She pressed her back against the cold wall. She couldn't face the grey paperwork and the Beadle's inevitable scorn at the job she would doubtless badly do.

What an imbroglio he's landed me in.

She closed her eyes. She thumped her head rhythmically. She chanted in her brain.

A. Po. Phax. A. Po. Phax. A. Po. Phax.

An itch nibbled under the skin of her left wrist. She scratched it with vicious will. It itched harder.

"Gah! Did I get bit by some weird space-moon-stairway-Fair bug?"

She had not been bit.

It was the loop of blue string. The one the Moirai had called 'Destiny Thread,' tying her to Apophax's sleeve. She had assumed he had undone it—along with whatever strange effects it had—when he'd yoinked his coat off her back.

It seemed not.

Curious.

The line wove three times round her wrist. Instead of disappearing up her sleeve (the way it had when the Moirai showed it to her), it dangled in empty space. She fancied a slight tug at the loose end, leading towards the window. She jerked her hand. Her wrist itched harder.

Is there more of it?

She let the thread lead her.

Tap… tap… tap…

Something—or someone—rapped on the shutters. Like they were testing them.

The Destiny Thread stretched through the wooden slats, like they weren't even there.

Some kind of immaterial extension cord?

The urge to scratch herself abated.

Impossible.

She pulled back. The string got taut.

WHOOM!

The unknown person pounded the shutters.

WHOOM! WHOOM! CRACK!

Madarena dove under the metal table.

BOOOOM!

The windows, frame and all, exploded inwards. Splinters of wood showered the room. Madarena barely covered her face in time. The table bore the brunt of the shrapnel.

Fresh white light flooded the room. A dark figure stood in the opening. He twirled a cane. He stepped lightly down from the shattered egress.

"Not the most conventional way to enter a room, I admit. However, I suspect I am persona entirely too non grata to use the front door of this particular establishment."

"APOPHAX!"

"Mine own inimitable self."

He brushed flecks of shutter dust off his shoulders.

Madarena had the presence of mind to check the Destiny Thread. Sure enough, though it looked like only a snippet of string, the end pointed straight at the wicked old grifter's wrist.

"AHA!"

She stood up, forgetting she was under the table.

"OW!"

She plonked down. She rubbed her head.

"What are you doing here?"

Apophax cleared his throat. He paced a slow circle around her.

"Imagine my surprise when, upon recovering my treasured coat in an unsavory alley exchange with a youthful hooligan, I went through my pockets and discovered a number of missing pieces of personal property."

"You had it coming."

He pointed one improbably long finger at her. "J'accuse!"

"There's no need to resort to French. I admit it. I stole your stuff."

The last intact piece of window frame gave up. It clonked to the floor. A cool breeze fluttered the strewn paperwork. Apophax drew himself up in a dignified pose.

"A lesser man would be sorely aggrieved by such abuse of his good nature."

"There are lesser men?"

"One hears rumors, yes. Which is neither here nor there."

He snapped his fingers imperiously.

"Come, come. Let us resolve the matter and we can part ways once more, putting this whole business behind us. No need to even involve the authorities, seeing as you have managed to get yourself locked up once again. Twice in less than twenty-four hours. Your parents must be proud."

He held out his open palm, expectantly.

Madarena emerged from the desk, on the opposite side. This was her chance. She said nothing. She was not one of those people who could arch an eyebrow—a personal failure she often regretted—so she had to make due with a sarcastic quirk of her lips.

"Oh come now! Don't tell me you already traded my things for candy or stickers or sparkling notions or whatever it is you hard-boiled adolescent women go for these days?"

He pressed his fingers to the bridge of his nose, quite melodramatically.

"Don't be asinine."

It was her turn to strut a circle around him.

"I believe the legal phrase," she rested a friendly hand carefully on his bequilled shoulder, "is quid pro quo."

"You're devilishly clever," grumbled Apophax. "It'll get you into trouble, by and by."

"I've read about the devil. He wishes he were clever as me."

"So it's come to this. Forced to seek legitimate redress for these importunities."

He put his fingers in the corners of his mouth, as if to whistle.

Madarena leaned on the desk. She crossed her arms.

"Please do. Summon the Logons. I'm sure they will take punitive action."

"I wirr," he growled around his fingers. "Don fink I wonn."

His chest expanded.

He did not whistle.

"I know you will. I'm sure of it. However..." she picked up a stray sheaf of gray paper. She idly folded it into an origami swan while talking. "If there's one thing I know about Logons, it's that they love rules. And I can only imagine that stolen property ends up in a big room somewhere, with labels and shelves and a couple stout Anubises watching it."

Apophax could not have looked more surprised if she'd turned into a newt. His hands fell slack at his side.

"In fact, I learned that from your plan! They'll take it to—what was the place on that business card? Interworld Property and Impoundment?"

His shoulders slumped. He coughed uncomfortably. He murmured something inaudible.

"What was that? Call Headmistress and Beadle? If you insist…"

"Alright, alright. You've made your point. What quid can I offer for your quo?"

"I want out of here."

He pointed Grimsykill's cane towards the shattered hole in the wall. "Thither."

"No. Not just out of the Strandhome. That's no good."

"I suppose not, given the alacrity with which you seek out incarceration." There wasn't a lot of heart in his jab. She pressed her advantage.

"I want free of Triskadeka Fair. And I want in on the Plan. Until you figure out a way to get me home."

The rogue's beetle-brow furrowed furiously, as if he brain-knitted a slew of objections.

The door opened.

Beadle appeared, carrying another stack of papers.

"What's all this?!"

"Run!" cried Apophax and Madarena at the same time.

He leapt over the table. He slid down a drainpipe.

"Unacceptable!" Beadle cried.

Madarena rushed him. She hit his pile of paperwork from underneath. A grey blizzard flew everywhere. It felt even more satisfying than she could've hoped.

"HEADMISTRESS! ANUBIS!"

Beadle grabbed at her. His shell-body proved too clumsy. She rolled to the windows. Apophax had just lighted to the ground.

"Wicked child!" Headmistress declared, arriving on the scene with a switch.

Hooting like a jackal, Madarena threw one last fistful of paperwork in the air.

"Sorted!"

She bowed. She shimmied down the drainpipe. Apophax had a good head start, but the bark of an Anubis at her back gave her wings. In no time, they raced neck-and-neck. Pell mell, they fled.

14.

They ended up crouched in a dark shed. They huddled together, ears pricked for sounds of pursuit. Madarena's lungs burned. Bright-colored dots swam in her eyes. Her breath sounded loud as crashing waves. She struggled to hold it shallow in her chest and make less sound.

After five minutes, Apophax sighed.

"Not caught yet, old boy," he said to himself. "And not a bad job of it by you as well, Miss Rua. You're a natural-born absconder."

"Thank you," she caught herself saying. She grew hot at the thought of being pleased by the rascal's praise.

"What now?" she asked to cover the moment.

"We were in the midst of delicate negotiations."

He cracked the shed door. Emboldened, he stepped outside.

They stood in a small statue garden behind a townhouse. The marble sculptures depicted creatures unlike any Madarena had seen, in myth or real life. Some looked like fat fish with too many fins and squiggly teeth, others had squids for heads perched on human bodies. A few were purely geometric forms made of corners that did not line up in the Euclidean way her eyes expected.

"Eldritch..." she whispered.

"Le mot juste." He sniffed the air. "Chthonons. Not the most felicitous wights to trespass against."

He peered at the stained-glass windows of the house. These showed strange scenes; tentacled things leering over impossible landscapes at masses of lesser beasts, fleeing.

"At least nobody's home. Now. Where were we?"

"Quid pro quo."

"Just so."

"So you'll do it? You'll take me with you?" She winced when she heard the eagerness in her own voice. *Poker face, girl.*

He plucked a loose thread off the Moirai's unfinished hoodie. "You may have potential..."

"How can someone *may* have potential? Isn't the whole point of potential that you have it or you don't?"

"You have the potential to have potential."

"Now you're being fiddly with words. Are you going to take me with you or not?"

"I suppose I've no choice. However, if you're going to be working for me—"

"—with you."

"Near me. In my general vicinity." He balanced a pair of pince-nez on the bridge of his nose. "Regardless, I should know a few things about you. Parents?"

"One of each kind. Living. Dull."

"Brothers or sisters?"

"Neither. I was deemed sufficient offspring."

"I've no doubt. Possibly more than sufficient. Age?"

"Young enough to be tried as a juvenile. In most jurisdictions."

"Good to know. Outstanding warrants?"

"None."

"Crimes for which you should have outstanding warrants but committed too cleverly to be accused?"

"None."

Unlike her, he could raise one eyebrow.

"That I know of," she added.

"I suppose it'll have to do. Any phobias? I don't want to get halfway through a scam and discover you're paralytically terrified of spiders or cheese or excessive lint on the lapel of a bespoke suit."

"Ennui."

"Please just answer. These are necessary questions no matter how boring you may find them."

"No. I meant, I have a phobia of ennui."

"A reasonable condition."

"That's what I think!"

Once again she found herself grudgingly liking Apophax the tiniest bit more.

He adjusted his pince-nez. "On to the value-add section of the interview. Do you possess any special abilities?"

She thought a moment. "Nothing springs to mind."

"Supernatural knacks?"

"No."

"Wizardry? Either via a credentialed institution or autodidactically?"

"No to either."

"Part of a special cadre of genetic mutants trained in secret by a shadowy organization called The Institute, Agency, or Collective?"

"Is that a thing?"

"Please just answer yes or no."

"No."

"No, 'you aren't going to answer in the binary' or no, 'you are not part of a mutant group'?"

"Yes."

"Hrm. Moving on. Nascent psychic powers waiting to be awakened by adolescence?"

"No."

"Ancestral tradition of magic that no one in the family talks about, which you're on the cusp of discovering within?"

"No."

"Ancestral tradition of magic that everyone in the family talks about nonstop, which you suspect you'll never awaken?"

"No."

"Favors owed you by ancient deities of unfathomable might?"

"Yes."

"Really?"

"No."

"You're not making a compelling case for yourself."

She shrugged.

"I'm a woman with a bad attitude and disreputable hoodie, who reads the dictionary for fun and has a deep fear of ennui. Take it or leave it."

"Very well." He held out a hand. "You may be my accomplice and I will take back my things."

She hesitated. "If I give you what you want, how do I know you won't conveniently forget to give me what I want?"

"Because for some reason, as yet unknown to me, my previous accomplice quit on me. Some twaddle about 'second thoughts' and 'time to move on'."

"Probably a good call on his part. It's a rough gig, I figure."

Apophax narrowed his eyes. She smiled back, innocent as a garden gnome amid the writhing eldritch statuary.

"At any rate, an accomplice is needed. At this late hour, I don't see anyone else lining up for the job."

"You're not making a very compelling case for yourself."

"I'm an old dream with a delightful demeanor and fancy coat, who built a fool-proof Plan and eschews all ennui. Take it or leave it."

She hesitated. Now that it came to the trade, she wasn't sure she wanted to give him the Plan. Not because of the Plan itself. Because of the sketch on the back. Aoede. The mystical, magical drawing that filled reality more fully than anything Madarena had known. And the music...

You'll never find the real her if you don't give up the drawing.

Resolved, she shook his outstretched hand.

She kicked off her slipper. He caught it mid-air. He wrinkled his nose. He fished the Plan out from the toe-box. As he did that, she handed over his passport and the Logon's business card.

"I used up the chalk," she reminded him as he returned her shoe.

"A bagatelle. You did what I was going to do with it anyway."

For the third time she found herself involuntarily pleased by something Apophax said. She resolved to be more vigilant against his praise.

She did not offer Planck's stopwatch. She figured the deal included only the possessions in his coat. And she wasn't going to give any bit of quid she didn't have to, to get her quo.

He did not seem to notice. He'd unfolded his plan. Her breath caught at the brief glance of Aoede before he tilted the page.

Don't worry. He won't get you, she vowed.

"Let's see... Triskadeka Jail... chalk face... bargain... Ah! Here we go." He jabbed a spot two-thirds of the way through the diagram. Madarena joined him.

"We're going to Thanatos?"

"How did you—?" He took a measured look at her. "Yes. That's correct. I'm surprised you can follow the thread. Not many can."

This time, she was ready. She ignored the compliment. "We're going to need passports."

"Just one. I'll be ensmallened in your pocket."

"To avoid facial recognition at the Logon kiosk?"

"Among other safeguards. I'm a hot item right now, in certain circles."

"Alright." She scanned the garden for an exit. "Let's go find the Rotwells before they leave town."

"The who-now?"

"You must have seen them. When you were casing the Strandhome."

"And you'd let these Rotwells be Stranded? Knowing that the Logons would take Daisy back to the Strandhome for whatever wretched task you were doing when I rescued you?"

"One: Paperwork. Two: My rescue was incidental. Three: Yes, yes I would."

He shook his head.

"So hard-boiled, so young."

"It's them or us." She pinned him with a gimlet eye. "And we're ever so much fonder of us, aren't we?"

"It sounds unsavory when you say it. Regardless—"

Apophax cleared his throat. Sleight of hand, he produced a mouldy booklet from behind a nearby statue's elephantine ear. In response to Madarena's wordless stare, he merely shrugged.

"I nicked young Daisy's passport as they walked out. One never knows what might come in handy. One just never knows."

"Imprecation."

"Let's go."

15.

"Over the back wall," the old thief's tiny, muffled voice directed from Madarena's pocket. "Straight on down the alley to the street. I'll tell you where from there."

She nipped nimbly up an enormous statue of a puffer fish, hard up against the wall. The big fish had a smaller puffer fish carved in its mouth, and an even smaller fish was carved inside that one's mouth. At the center of the three fish was a tiny fisherman, his line hooked onto the biggest fish's lip and tangled round his own legs. The fisherman's eyes bulged out of their sockets and his mouth was frozen open in a silent cry of terror.

As she clambered by, Madarena shuddered in spite of herself. Whatever came next, she would be glad to be out of Triskadeka Fair.

Guided by Apophax's whispers from her pocket, Madarena made her way to Orrery Square. The rope maze had shifted. Since last she'd been there, the slow tick of the Orrery had moved the COSMOS sphere out of the light. Instead, THANATOS glowed on a different ring.

She had expected the Thanatons to all be zombies like the Rotwells. Instead, she saw a panoply of undead creatures, coming out of the light and waiting to go back in.

There were zombies, to be sure, shuffling and moaning. She also saw translucent ghosts, floating docilely in the two queues. Red-eyed wights with teeth filed to points jostled shoulders with bone-mumbling ghouls. A crisply wrapped mummy dragged an upright sarcophagus behind him on a two-wheeled dolly, tapping one foot every time the line stopped moving.

She even spotted a vampire girl. The pale young woman was a bit older than herself. Mouth slightly agape (displaying her pointy teeth), she stared vacantly at her sparkly nails with the dullest expression Madarena had ever seen.

"Oh, get over yourself," Madarena muttered.

"Don't dawdle!" Apophax whispered emphatically. "Get in line and let's get this done."

"Shush you. Don't get us caught."

Unlike earlier, the rope maze thronged. All of the kiosks were occupied by Logon shells, stamping stacks of papers, checking passports, asking a series of rote questions and barely listening to the answers, and generally slowing everyone's progress down as much as legally permissible.

Of course. There would *be a line.*

She fell in behind a dripping sea ghast with skin of green.

He carried a large clear bag, filled with brackish water. In it floated one of the squidish creatures that Madarena recognized from the statue garden. She could not tell whether it was alive or dead or maybe just sleeping. The ghast smelled like the beach at low tide, when all the dead fish in the sea bake rotting in the sun.

A pair of desiccated corpses dressed in ornately printed silks hopped up behind her. One clutched a gold flute between its blue-lacquered fingernails. The other held the neck of a five-stringed tortoise-shell lute. Their jet black hair was pulled back into tight ponytails that flapped when they jumped. Once in line, they bounced slightly up and down in place, waiting their turn.

"Are you sure this is a good idea?" she whispered to wee Apophax.

"Shush," it was his turn to say. "No way out but through. And remember—you're supposed to be Daisy Rotwell. It wouldn't hurt to groan a bit and shuffle."

Madarena wanted to object, but she couldn't disagree with him. Holding Daisy's passport, she moaned from time to time, and shuffled forward whenever the line moved.

The ghast leaked a steady stream of salt water, so her slippers were soaked before she was even halfway to the kiosk.

"This is so ugh. I want new slippers when this is all over."

"That seems like your problem to solve. Focus."

Sick of squishing with every step, she kicked off the waterlogged moccasins. It was gross to walk through the ghast-puddles, but grosser still to steep her feet in that nasty stuff. She nudged them to the side of the line with one foot and a shudder, leaving them behind.

When she looked up from the ground, her petty worries of foot rot and ghast water fled. Across the Square, she saw Chironex and Grimsykill. And, worse still, they saw her.

Chironex waved her long razors. A shiver shot down Madarena's spine. The killers made a bee-line for her across the plaza. A train of skeletons, each carrying a different instrument, marched out of the light cone directly across their path.

Flexing his powerful shoulders, Grimsykill shoved them this way and that, sending their bones tumbling apart in a great chaotic mess. While the three skeletons still standing tried to piece their bandmates back together, the two assassins stalked on.

Madarena glanced every which way. She did not want to flee the Square—where would she go from there? The line crawled forward. She stood two spots from the kiosk.

"May I go ahead of you?" she asked the ghast. "I have an appointment to keep."

The ghast merely leered at her with eyes that pointed in different directions. He burbled something and held up the bag with the weird fish-like thing in it, and burbled some more.

"Alright, alright."

Suddenly, Grimsykill was there beside her.

"I believe," he snarled, "I owe you a murdering."

He reached out two enormous hands towards her throat. A cold part of Madarena's brain thought *Don't give him the satisfaction of a scream.* Another part thought *I hope no one is too sad back home.* A third part shouted *RUN!* but her legs would not move. A feeble moan escaped her as she felt a wave of cold from his throttling fingers, waggling towards her neck.

"The line," said a voice, dry as dust in a desert that had never seen rain, *"begins this way. Please follow me."*

An Anubis formed from the plaza ground. It swirled up behind Grimsykill and Chironex, dwarfing both of them. Madarena squeaked in relief.

"We have business with this little one," Chironex said, unctuously.

"The line begins this way. Please follow me."

"NO!"

Grimsykill lunged at Madarena, flecks of spittle on his lips.

The Anubis seized him by both shoulders, stopping him dead in his tracks, a scant centimeter from her neck.

"The line begins this way. Please follow me."

Another Anubis had joined the first. She took Chironex by the arm and repeated the instruction.

Helpless, the killers eye-murdered Madarena.

"The line," she pointed with an insouciant smirk, "begins that way. Please follow them."

The sea ghast moved up. Following, Madarena watched over her shoulder as the Anubises dragged the killers far, far to the back of the line.

Once there, Grimsykill pulled himself loose of the Anubis's grip. He smoothed out his suit coat. He stood in his place, seemingly content to wait. The moment the Anubises turned their backs, he sprinted towards Madarena. Both guards turned to clouds of dust, whirled past the black blur that was Grimsykill and reformed right in front of Madarena. Once more, they seized the murderous thug.

"You have been politely asked," the man-Anubis said. *"Now you will come with us."*

Together, they frog-marched the cursing Grimsykill out of the Square. Madarena watched with some satisfaction (and no little fear, still, even after he was gone). After he disappeared, she looked over to Chironex, still in line.

The assassin drew one bladed forearm across her throat. She stepped out of line. She did not pursue—just watched from deep within her poison-green cowl.

One of the hopping corpses behind Madarena nudged her. She realized that the ghast had moved on to the Stair, leaving the fish-monster (still in its bag) behind on the Logon's desk.

"Passport."

Remembering to moan and shuffle, Madarena handed him Daisy's passport.

"Purpose of visit?"

"Vuuurrrcccaaahhhshun." She hoped her zombie impersonation was credible. The Logon did not seem to care.

"Anything to declare?"

"Nnnuhhhh."

She never understood why they asked the question. If someone *were* smuggling something (like a miniscule wanted criminal), the answer would still be no.

"Did you purchase anything during your visit?"

"Nnnnuhhh."

This went on for quite some time. After all the questions on his list had been answered, the Logon (who had not even bothered to look at her, the whole time), waved Madarena past.

As quickly as she dared, she shuffled to the circle of light. The surge of safety she felt was quickly extinguished, however. The last thing she saw before stepping onto the Lichgate Stair was Chironex, across the Square, tracking her with an implacable glare.

16.

The hubbub cut off the second she put her first foot on the moonlight stair. She paused amid a silent sea of pinpoint stars. The steps glowed translucent beneath her, descending into the void.

"Hurry on then," Apophax said in a muffled voice from deep within her pocket.

"There was a long line on the other side. Where'd they all go?"

With a grunt, Apophax wriggled out of his cloth prison. He frowned up at her. "You can have explanations or you can have an escape. Which will it be?"

"Alright, alright. No need to get impatient."

She carefully made her way down the Lichgate Stair. Sixty steps down, she saw a smoky grey dot far below, hovering against the obsidian sky. Seventy steps down, the marble grew to a globe of swirling mist as big as Grimsykill's fist. Eighty steps. A cloud-bound sphere the size of Orrery Square loomed beneath her. Ninety steps. The curve of Thanatos's foggy horizon eclipsed half the stars in the sky.

On the one hundredth step, she alighted onto a cold slab of granite.

She stood at the base of a badly corroded street lamp. A puddle of weak greenish light seethed over her bare feet. The faint scent of decay crawled up her nose. She peered into the thick fog. She couldn't see more than a finger's length. She pricked her ears. Muffled creaks of antique cars and the shuffle of hundreds of feet filled the air—a town of decent size. Water slapped a pier somewhere nearby.

Apophax hoisted himself out of her pocket. He flipped end over end, tucking and rolling through the air.

"Wait!"

Too late.

She'd lost him again. Or he'd ditched her.

"Imprecation!"

She searched for a clue as to where to go next. A rust-spotted street sign on the lamp-post read:

RESPICE POST TE BLVD

She couldn't believe she'd made the mistake of trusting Apophax. She really had thought he needed an accomplice, that she had him in a bind.

"Feh."

"What was that?"

Right-sized again, he emerged from the fog.

"Nothing."

No need to let him know he'd worried her.

"An appropriate sentiment for the place. Welcome to Charonsferry, a minor port of call in the vast and distinctly dead world of Thanatos."

He squinted at the street sign through a pair of reading cheaters.

"Tsh, tsh, tsh." He tapped the frame of the glasses on his teeth. "We want to get to Ubi Sunt Lane. If memory serves…"

"You've been here before?"

"Once," he replied, with a faraway look. It might have been the gloomy light or the gothy odors, but Madarena fancied she caught sadness in his stare.

"Running from something?"

She instantly regretted the levity. Apophax didn't seem to notice. As quick as it had caught him, the moody moment let him go. With a smile that was a touch too sincere, he rapped Grimsykill's cane on the granite sidewalk.

"Neither here nor there, accomplice. Neither here. Nor there."

Without further ado, he swept into the mist. She followed in his wake.

"I want to introduce you to some friends of mine. A friend in particular. Chap who, like us, isn't from around here. He does, however, owe me a very old quo."

Strange shapes passed them by. Some walked like people. Some lurched. Some floated. The haze obscured them all.

"Do things work that way even after you're dead? Quid pro quo, I mean."

"After?"

She lowered her voice. She jerked her head at the passersby. "You know. After."

She didn't want a repeat of when she'd been rude to the Chronons by asking for a moment of their time. Maybe pointing out the people all around her were dead was a faux pas.

"Ah. You've misunderstood. Thanatos is not where people go who were once living and are now dead. It is where people who were never anything but dead are from."

"What about the people who were once living and are now dead?"

"They," Apophax grimly replied, "are gone."

That made Madarena unsure and sad and strangely light-headed all at once. Pensive introspection displaced her curiosity. She allowed Apophax to herd her with nudges of his cane through the shrouded streets.

Once on Ubi Sunt Lane, he led her to a large sandstone edifice. The lichen-spotted walls reminded her of the church on Peabody Street, back on Earth. The memory of it—with the cemetery and the Lichgate Stair—felt decades off. So far gone, it might as well have happened to someone else.

"Hup hup!" Apophax's jaunty summons pulled her out of the reverie.

They left the street. Pea gravel crunched under their feet. A rusting iron fence marked the path. Thick red beads coagulated off the fence. Madarena marveled it did not just dissolve in front of her eyes.

The walkway ended at the warped oak door of a squat, ramshackle house. Using the head of Grimsykill's cane, Apophax tapped an elegiac couplet on the wood. He leaned back on his heels. He whistled a mournful snatch of melody.

The door did not open.

"They must be out. No matter. I know where the spare key is."

He made a great show of lifting the corner of the tattered reed doormat. His clever fingers twitched. He held a curious key, comprised of two long, thin tines.

It looked to Madarena like there'd been nothing beneath the mat. Indeed, it looked exactly like Apophax had produced the so-called spare key by plucking two quills from his coat.

She held her peace. There was no point in calling him on it. Besides, she'd never seen someone pick a lock. It might be a useful skill to learn.

He put the 'key' into the lock. He jiggled it about. Madarena leaned in for a closer look. With a soft *click* the door swung open on groaning hinges.

"Ok, I missed that. Can you do it again?"

He gave her the picks.

"Try it yourself."

She wasn't as nimble as him. It took five tries with patient coaching. In the end, she managed. She offered him the quills back.

"Keep them," he said with a mentorial wave of his hand. "I've more."

She pinned them inside her hoodie. She couldn't wait to practice. This *would* be an extremely useful skill.

Belying its outward hovelish appearance, his friends' home was quite cozy and well-appointed. Intricately woven wool rugs covered every square centimeter of floor, piled deep. Madarena hadn't realized how cold and sore her bare feet were till they sank into the lush comfort.

A low fire smoldered in the main room's wood stove. A spiral staircase in one corner led down. A hallway, beyond a tassel door of tiger-eye beads, exited to the back of the house. Paintings—still lifes of rotten fruit and forlorn landscapes devoid of figures—decorated the walls. Two overstuffed leather chairs, each with its own ottoman, faced the stove. Several oil lamps shed sufficient light to make the room positively cheery, especially when compared to the vaporous gloom outside.

"See if you can't coax a bit more warmth from the fire," Apophax ordered her. "I'll go see what our hosts have in the way of hospitality."

Madarena pulled an ottoman in front of the stove. She stoked the coals with a poker. Apophax disappeared through the tassel door. From the rattle of dishes and bang of cupboard doors down the hall, she presumed he looted the kitchen.

"These friends of yours," she called out, "who are they?"

"The habit," Apophax harumphed over the roar of water filling a kettle, "of asking too many questions is one of your most appealing qualities. Unusual in a Cosmon."

"That's another thing! I thought there were billions of worlds around billions of stars. Are there only thirteen? When did that happen? Who decided?"

The floodgates of curiosity opened. Questions poured out.

"And where is Triskadeka Fair? Is it in the middle of a bunch of planets no one can see? How does it work? Why are the Logons in charge? Who made it? Why does the Lichgate—"

"Peace, peace, rest in peace!"

Apophax returned with a tray of cookies, crackers, assorted green and blue cheeses, and a tea service of exceedingly tasteful china.

"Let the water boil first."

He set the tray on an end table. He assembled himself a plate of cookies. He plopped into a leather chair and stretched his spindly legs onto the corresponding ottoman. He rested the plate on his belly. He nibbled a sugar wafer.

"Please, please." He waved the last bite at the tray of food. "No need to stand on ceremony. Take, eat, be merry."

Madarena bored holes into him with her eyes.

"Very well, very well. But I'm going to eat while you grill me. I haven't had a decent meal in an Aeon's age."

"Triskadeka Fair," she said, plucking a topic at random from the many that swirled around in her head. "What is it? Why does it look familiar except not?"

"The thing about Triskadeka Fair," Apophax replied, between bites of jam-sandwich shortbread, "is... or rather, isn't... the thing, I mean... Well, talking about Triskadeka Fair is like the blind men and the elephant. You know the one?"

She, in fact, did. It was an old story.

"Several blind men found an elephant," she recited. "One felt her trunk and said she was a snake. Another felt her leg and said she was a tree, a third felt her tusk and said she was a rock and so on. They argued about what she was and—"

"—and the elephant trampled them all to death. Because what self-respecting pachyderm is going to stand for being groped by a bunch of bickering blind men?"

"You are without a doubt the least helpful old man anywhere, ever."

Apophax's retort was lost. At that moment, two things happened. First, the tea kettle screamed in the kitchen. Second, with the front door's rattle and groan, their unknowing hosts came home.

17.

Madarena had expected the home's owners to be some sort of undead, so she was taken aback when a tall, thin, stern man who looked very much alive strode into the living room.

He was her father's age, with a bit of grey around his blond temples and crow's-feet around his piercing blue eyes. His face was a symmetry of narrow angles that might have been disconcertingly sharp, had he not carried it off with such confidence. He wore a full-length black cassock with a high, stiff collar.

He stopped in his tracks when he saw Apophax. He did not look pleased.

"We have visitors, Jack," he called back to the foyer in a low growl, never taking his eyes off the old man in his leather chair. "No need to put yourself out. They seem to have helped themselves."

"What's that? Can't hear you over the kettle racket," came the strained reply. "I didn't leave it on, did I?"

An enormous stack of parcels, with two bow-legs wobbling beneath it, struggled into the room.

"Don't mind, I've got it all," the second man wheezed from behind his precariously piled burdens. He surged further into the room, towards the kitchen hall.

Unfortunately, he did not see Madarena in his way. His boot clipped the tip of her toe.

"OW!" she cried, for her feet were still bare.

The tower of packages tumbled.

"Down I go!" cried the man behind.

Oddly shaped fruits and nuts with mottled purple shells spilled out all over the carpet and under the furniture. A puff of pinkish flour filled the air. Several wheels of cheese rolled free into the hallway.

As the package-carrying man grabbed at the end table to stop his fall, he upended the tea tray. A barrage of sticky cheese bits flung from the tray and stuck to the far wall. Most of the cookies hit the carpet in a burst of crumbs, but Apophax did manage to nimbly snatch one out of the air as he sat up and set his plate to the side.

When the chaos settled out, Madarena's toe throbbed, bright red, in tune to the screaming kettle. Apophax nibbled a sugar-dusted almond snap, returning the host's ice-blue stare with wide-eyed insouciance. The package-man lay sprawled full-length on the floor.

"I am so sorry!" Madarena exclaimed.

"No harm done!"

Now that she could see him, free of parcels, she realized that he, at least, was probably a Thanaton. He looked to be composed (or perhaps, she thought, *de*composed) primarily of animal bones, potato peels, fruit pith, and cheese rinds — in short, all the cast-offs of a kitchen garbage heap. Despite this, it was *he* who looked at *her* with shock.

"Compost me! There's something you don't see every day."

He reached out a chicken-bone finger (wrapped in apple skin) and poked her pulsing big toe.

"Oy!" she yelped, pulling her foot back.

"Well that's a marvel for the midden. Oof, now where are my manners?" He stood up and offered her his hand. "Kitchen Jack, at your service, Miss."

Without waiting to see if she'd take him up on the offer (or even take his hand), he looked round at the mess.

"Tea kettle!"

He dashed down the hall. The screaming ceased. Wanting to be helpful, Madarena set to cleaning things up. She found it hard to pay attention to the task while also eavesdropping on the conversation.

"What brings you from Ivorygate, Apophax?" asked the man in the black cassock, who had never once, in all of the chaos, taken his gaze from the intruder.

"Not to impose myself on you, *von Katzen*, rest assured."

Madarena suspected he emphasized the other man's name for her benefit, and she made a note of it. Apophax continued.

"Since, it seems, we're skipping pleasantries, I need to see your sister."

"Ah," von Katzen replied with a little clipped sound. "I am afraid I will not be of much help then. Mouldywarp—"

Another name from the Plan! Madarena dropped the packages she had been carefully piling in her arms. With a smile at the two contesting men, she said "Whoops. Careless me."

"Stop, stop," said Kitchen Jack, returning from the kitchen. "Do let me."

He gathered up the last of the parcels. Madarena retrieved one of the china plates. She peeled the various cheeses off of the wall and did her best to pick crumbled cookies out of the carpet, while still listening in.

"—Mouldywarp," von Katzen resumed, "has gone to ground, some time since. Perhaps," he finished with a small, superior smile in his voice that did not show on his lips, "she knew you were coming."

"I had…" Apophax paused to stretch his limbs all in the same direction, yawning casual as a cat. Relaxing again, he continued, "…anticipated that. Naturally I—or rather, we—need a place to stay until I find her."

"Dross and dreck, Apophax!" Kitchen Jack said, "Of course you and your remarkable little friend are welcome in our house any time. Thank you, miss," he finished, as Madarena stacked the last of his strewn packages high atop the pile in his arms.

She would not have thought it possible for von Katzen to stare more intensely at Apophax, nor stand more stock still. She would have been wrong.

"Jack, dear," he said, barely moving his lips, "please take Apophax's… whatever she is… to the kitchen and offer her some dinner."

Balancing the parcels, Kitchen Jack gestured with his head towards the hall. "This way, if you please."

With some reluctance (for she wanted nothing more than to hear the details of what she assumed would be a grand ensuing argument), Madarena followed him out of the room.

The last thing she heard was Apophax saying, with avuncular modesty: "My accomplice Madarena. Such a good child, isn't she? Such a help."

Von Katzen's only answer was a low tomcat growl. As soon as Madarena stepped into the hall, the rest of the conversation fell muffled, as though a wool blanket had been thrown over her head.

18.

Kitchen Jack insisted she sit while he put away the groceries. Madarena perched on a three-legged stool. Instead of restocking the pantry, he just stared at her.

"What?"

She felt a bit defensive, being ogled by a man made of food scraps.

"Begging your pardon. I'm just a simple Charonsferry kobenhold, but you are, right if I am, living? Proper-like living?"

"Yes…"

She was unsure exactly why that would merit such unabashed childish enthusiasm.

"Right alive? Not a dream? Or hollow as a Logy?"

Without so much as a do-you-mind, he rapped her forehead with squishy orange rind knuckles.

"Oy!" She hopped back off the stool. "Space!"

With a delighted giggle, Jack danced over to a drawer. He pulled out a large steel ladle.

"Here." He held it up in front of her face. "Breathe on this."

The kobenhold's face was so sincere, with its potato skin grin and glistening avocado pit eyes, she couldn't help but comply. She huffed a breath onto the ladle. Kitchen Jack leaned in close. He squeed with glee at the condensation, swiftly evaporating from the mirrored metal.

"Again!"

She obliged.

"Trashbits! That's just magic. Magic is what that is. Once more, maybe?"

"Alright," she said, benevolently. "Just the once more. I don't want to spoil the effect by over-use."

He shook his head in wonder as her breath steamed up the steel again.

"Didn't Mister von Katzen ask you to offer me some dinner?" She hoped to distract him. She *was* hungry, and did not want to spend all night breathing on a spoon.

"That he did!" He rummaged around. "He's a good host, really, though he doesn't like surprises. Not at all."

"I don't think he'll let us stay long."

"Trash and toss-offs! Sure he will. Your uncle is always welcome here."

He stopped pulling together food. His wrinkly-food face scrunched up fondly. He sighed.

"He was the one who introduced Wilhelm and me. That he was."

"Dinner?" Madarena prodded.

Kitchen Jack came back to the moment. "Right, right, right! What do the living eat, anyway?"

"What does Mister von Katzen eat?"

"Usually I make up a mess of chicken and rice, with some clams all mashed up in it. Twice a day. He doesn't care for fancy fare."

That did not sound promising to Madarena. However, it at least sounded edible, which she was not sure anything else in this world of ghouls might be.

"That would be fine, I'm sure."

As he set to chopping chicken, she continued the conversation. "So Apophax introduced you two?"

"Yes indeed. And at our wedding, I said to him, after the toasts and halfway through the dancing, I said 'You are always welcome in our home.'"

He measured out some jasmine rice and started the water to boil.

"And that's why I know you'll be staying as long as he wants."

"Why is Mister von Katzen so angry with him?"

"What makes you say that?"

It seemed Kitchen Jack had completely missed the tension in the living room.

"They didn't exactly greet each other like old friends. No handshakes or hugs."

"That's just his way. He's not one much for displays."

He tossed the diced chicken into a pan with a little oil. Madarena's stomach answered the sizzling and smell with a loud growl.

"They hardly even nodded hello."

"Pish. I'm sure by now they're chatting away like two ragmen in a wagon."

That, Madarena certainly did not believe. But she let the matter lie. If Kitchen Jack was too pleasant to notice conflict, who was she to disillusion him?

Changing the subject, she asked: "Have you known Apophax a long time?"

"Not so long as my husband has, that's sure. A while, though." He pulled a can of diced clams down from a shelf. "Stir that, dear, would you?"

Madarena scraped the chicken off the bottom of the pan and stirred it up to keep it from burning.

"What was he like?"

"He was so suave and polite. He stepped right out of my dreams, charming as you please, and said 'Good day, sir.'"

"I didn't mean von Katzen," She noticed the water boiling, and took it upon herself to dump the rice in. "I meant Apophax."

"That's who I was talking about!" He leaned over her shoulder and dumped the whole can of clams onto the chicken. "Snags and rags, he was a charmer in those days."

"Really?"

It was hard for her to imagine Apophax as suave, let alone 'charming as you please.'

"Sure as slurry." He stood next to her and stirred the boiling rice with a wooden spoon. "He was quite the matchmaker too. And—" here he paused, as if revealing something a touch wicked, "—a bit of a gadabout, or so I hear."

"What do you mean?" She lifted a piece of chicken and pried it apart to check for doneness. It was cooked perfectly. She scarfed it down.

"He was always going somewhere or coming back from somewhere."

"Well, that much hasn't changed."

He turned off the rice burner.

"Excuse me, Miss."

Madarena sat down at the kitchen table to get out of his way. He scraped the rice into a bowl and added the chicken and clams.

"He never stayed one place long enough to do more than make people want him to stay a whole lot longer."

"I bet." She remembered the Judge at Triskadeka Jail. "People do seem to want him to stick around."

"And he never would, poor fellow. But now he's not all alone! He's got you to keep him company! And you're wicked smart and magic fun."

"I'm one of those four things. Two on a good day."

He flashed with a lovely corn-toothed smile. He vigorously stirred the rice, chicken, and clams together.

"Don't be modest! Everyone needs good company, and I'm glad he found his."

To her surprise, Madarena found herself blushing.

"What's *that* you're doing?" Kitchen Jack exclaimed. He touched her cheek. "Are you ripening, right here and now?"

The harder she tried not to blush, the redder and hotter she got. "No—just—it's—" Under the kobenhold's innocent scrutiny, she found herself at a loss for words.

Von Katzen's appearance at the kitchen door saved her. His thin lips pressed tight together. He looked as though he had swallowed something half-rotten and were waiting for it to all-the-way spoil in his stomach.

Apophax, a touch under half his host's height, peeked around the black cassock. He winked at Madarena and tapped his nose.

"Dear," von Katzen said to Kitchen Jack, "when Apophax's accomplice has eaten, could you please set her up in the guest bedroom? We will return shortly."

"Heaps of glee!" the kobenhold cried, and spooned a dollop of mush onto her plate.

19.

While Madarena ate, Kitchen Jack excused himself to prepare the guest room. She was glad for some time to herself. She had a great deal more to digest than chicken mashed with rice and clams.

The kobenhold made the second person since Planck who got stars in their eyes when talking about Apophax. There must be more to the hedgehog-coated thief than a long list of outrages and felonies.

In fact, the only people who disliked him were the same kinds of people who disliked her. Authority figures. Fusspots. Mean girls.

Grimsykill and Chironex.

The shiver in her bones had nothing to do with the grim scrape of the spoon on the bottom of her bowl.

Yes. Them.

She needed to figure out a way to steal that Aoede figurine without leaving Apophax dangling for the Night Mayor's assassins. He didn't deserve killing.

If you steal her though, won't they come after you?

The dry mocking voice had a good point.

If Apophax had a plan, the Night Mayor had a counter-plan. She needed to derail both.

Oh. Just that? No problem. And then ransack Fort Knox and the Louvre on your way home.

Shut up.

She brooded at the empty bowl. The conundrum flummoxed her.

"I don't know enough!"

"None of us do," Kitchen Jack piped, bustling back into the kitchen. "Except maybe my husband. Middens, I swear, some days Willie knows everything there is to know."

He cleared the table. He continued talking over the sound of washing up. "Of course your friend Apophax is no slouch either."

"He's not my friend."

"No? What is he then?"

She did not have a word. She settled for a noncommittal grunt.

Her host stacked the dishes in the drying rack. He wiped his hands on his oil-stained shirt.

"Whatever he is, I'm sure between them they can sort your troubles out."

She pushed her chair back. She stood up.

"I think I need to work this one out on my own."

"Of course you do. Self-reliant. Like both of them. Still... isn't it nice to have help now and again?"

"I wouldn't know."

"Rubbish! Everyone gets help now and again."

"Not me."

"If you say so. I suppose someone who can breathe fog doesn't need much more than that."

He led her down the hall. He nattered on, giving her a tour of his home. Her mood turned gloomy. Far from lifting her spirits, Kitchen Jack's bright patter cast shadows on her brain. She was alone and had to figure out what to do, which might be impossible. Her least favorite IM word.

"And here's where you'll be resting."

The guest room lay below ground. Rain tapped against one window, high in the corner. A rosewood coffin took up most of the space. Kitchen Jack had thoughtfully piled many blankets and pillows in the silk-lined box. A candle-topped skull on the bedside table provided the only guttering light.

"Thank you."

"Now if you're needing anything just call me and let me know."

"I will."

"I'm serious! I don't know what a living body might want nor need without you telling me. So promise."

His earnestness broke through her mood, just a bit. She raised an open palm and nodded.

"Alright. I promise." As he turned to leave, she asked: "Maybe a pair of shoes or socks? My feet are freezing."

"I'll see what I can dig up!"

"It can wait till morning, no worries."

"Good night till then, Madarena."

"Good night."

She listened for his footsteps down the hall. She checked the door. Unlocked. On tip-toes, she unlatched the single window. It squeaked open enough for her to wriggle through, if needs must. She was not trapped.

That settled, she luffed most of the pillows and blankets to the floor. She crawled into the coffin. The padding proved surprisingly comfy. Being cradled by the snug rosewood frame soothed her more than she would've guessed.

She wrapped herself up in a woolen shroud that smelled of cloves and ginger. She fluffed a dusty down bolster under her head. She pulled her hood low over her eyes.

Right, let's figure what Apophax —

A gust from the window snuffed the candle. Sleep drowned her thoughts before she finished the sentence.

20.

She surfaced from a warm ocean of unconsciousness into a hedge-walled den.

What on Earth?

The thought echoed in an odd fashion. Or rather, she thought it several times at slightly different moments.

She stood up.

And then she stood up.

And then she stood up again.

Each time was a little different. First she pushed herself to standing. The second time, she hopped to her feet like an acrobat. The third time, she paused in a careful crouch before reaching her full height.

What is going on?

Her body buzzed. Her mind too—as though her thoughts were queued up on a delay, or like they were badly over-dubbed.

Disconcerted, she waved her hand in front of her face. Several hands, in sequence, traced a path before her eyes. The sight nauseated her.

Let's not do that.

No more of that.

Yerk.

All the thoughts happened simultaneously, yet somehow she thought each one as though it were all 'she' were thinking. She'd never cogitated in parallel before. Not a pleasant adjustment.

Her surroundings, by contrast to her appearance, presented a still and singular vision. The ground pressed her multitude of bare feet with reassuring stability. She focused on these externals until the queasy feeling receded.

She'd woken midst thickets of thorny bushes. They loomed and curved, blocking the sky. A musty smell filled the air—like an animal's den. Small yellow electric lights had been strung along the branches. In the dim glow, she spotted a single sharp quill, sticking out of the dirt. Half of her seized it.

Aha!

J'accuse.

How are you here?

Of course it's you.

Apophax.

Narrow passages ran between the hedges. To her left and right they branched into more passages.

Hedge maze.

Labyrinth.

Trap.

Tangle.

Web.

Topiary escape room.

Stop that, all of you.

She struggled to calm the tumult of the various Madarenas, all thinking slightly different things at once.

Can we all agree on getting out of here?

Let's get out of here.

Let's go.

On we go.

Solve the maze.

Always turn right.

Always turn left.

Alternate left and rights.

STOP!

It was like trying to ride a dozen boats at the same time, in the middle of a storm, and none of them heading to the same destination. Bewildering. Whatever this strange place was doing to her brain, she needed it to stop.

She strode down the passage to her left—aware that another version of her (or was it her? So confusing!) went right. At the next intersection, they split again. And on and on.

Each time the path branched, two new Madarenas walked both roads at once. Very quickly, they—she—all the shes—multiplied beyond count. She lost all sense of which one was the 'real' her and which the copy.

In a cloud of potential, she wandered the maze.

One of her reached the first dead end. She sprinted back to the last intersection. All of the other Madarenas stopped hard when the Dead End Girl reached the last common turning point and—without warning—disappeared.

Imprecation!

Collapse!

Perhaps...

However she got there, all the versions of her agreed: When there was no further decision to be made, that Madarena was pruned out of existence.

A few of her panicked at the thought. In the main, she decided it was for the best and over-ruled the handful of objectors. She paced deliberately forward, down all the paths at once.

Dead end after dead end whittled away at her possible selves. She turned the last corner onto a vast verdant meadow. In a trice, all remaining possibilities stepped into the muddy feet of the first Madarena to find the exit. With that, she stood singular again.

Across the meadow, she spotted a hedgehog. His hands clasped behind his back. He craned his neck to stare up. An alabaster statue towered over him—her face the spit and image of the sketch on the back of his Plan.

"Oh, Muse, Muse, my dearest Muse..." he sighed.

Aoede wore flowing yellow and red robes. She cradled a rosewood dulcimer between her deft brown hands. If the sketch had struck Madarena as beyond life-like, the statue filled space so fully as to make 'life-like' too weak an adjective for anything else.

Despite that, the Muse did not move.

She was more real than real. Yet that was not enough.

"Who is she?" Madarena whispered.

Startled, Apophax whirled. Tears shone in his black eyes and streaked his cheeks. When he saw it was Madarena, the grief twisting his face turned to mirth.

"Accomplice! I knew you had potential."

Before she could react, Kitchen Jack shook her out of the dream.

21.

"Whatdyadothafur?" she slurred, prying open sleep-crusted eyes.

Rain-grey dawn filtered into the guest room through gauze curtains. Sullen patter tapped the glass.

Kitchen Jack hovered solicitously over her.

"Time for breakfast. And here, look what I dug up!"

He capered back, unable to contain helpful glee. He held up a pair of black, flat-heel boots and a deep purple dress.

"I got you some day clothes as well. I hope you don't mind. Was that right? It seemed right."

The last bits of sleep fled. In the room next door, she heard Apophax snort a mighty morning snort.

"Yes, of course. Thank you. I love the color."

When she rose, he held it up to her. "A perfect fit, if I do say so. Now you change and come get breakfast."

The long-sleeve calf-length dress fit perfectly. The boots could've been cobbled for her. Both articles smelled of the same musty decay that pervaded the whole of Thanatos. She decided it would be best not to wonder if Jack had literally meant 'dug up'.

She re-donned the muslin hoodie she'd pinched from the Moirai. As she did so, she remembered the strange multiplicity of her dream. She concentrated.

I'll go to breakfast.

I won't go to breakfast.

Both thoughts were thought one after the other by the same her—the definite article, as she'd told Headmistress.

That's more like it.

She stepped into the hall. The door of the next room hung slightly ajar. Within she heard whuffles, grunts, and scrapes.

Time for some explanations.

Without bothering to knock, she breezed in. Apophax squatted in the midst of ridiculous calisthenics. He called out the exercises as he did them.

"Huff! Upright! Accomplice! Ho! Leg thrust! I trust! Hup! Squat! You passed! Huff! Upright! A pleasant! Ho! Side twist! Night! Hup! Squat!"

"Tolerable. Odd dreams."

"You! Huff! Upright! Don't! Ho! Back bend! Say!"

"Was any of that real? It felt real. Not like a dream."

He paused. Winded, he toweled the sweat off his head.

"If you can avoid getting old, I'd recommend it," he said. "This used to be easy."

"Would it kill you to just answer a question?"

"Depends on the question."

She glowered. He sprinted in place for forty-five seconds, knees high. As he did, he said:

"Your query is ill-formed. Real and dream are not binary opposites."

"How's that work?"

He stretched his arms over his head and grabbed his toes. For all his grumbles about the ravages of age, she thought, he was remarkably limber.

"Don't know. Didn't do it."

Kitchen Jack tapped her on the shoulder.

"Eggs are getting cold."

The heady aroma of eggs, sausage, and toast wafted down the hall. Evidently someone had told Jack there was more to living-person food than clam-and-rice mash.

"Go ahead. I'm going to finish my exercises and wash up."

Once again, Madarena tried splitting herself to accommodate both choices. It did not work. Mostly because even if she'd managed to leave one of her to wrangle answers out of the old man, that one's stomach would've gone with the others.

She inhaled a hearty meal, much to Kitchen Jack's delight. The alacrity with which she ate proved insufficient. Brimful of calories and questions, she hurried back to Apophax's room.

Empty as an unused tomb.

Gauze curtains billowed. The ozone odor of rain wafted down. A chair below the window told the whole story.

"Blast it, Apophax!"

She climbed up the chair and outside.

The weather had worsened. She couldn't see more than five meters. Waterfilled footprints headed off at a long stride across the muddy graveyard.

"Blast it, blast it, blast it!"

She squelched across the cemetery. When she reached the wrought-rust fence, the footprints disappeared. It was useless. He knew how to cover his tracks. He had a head start and, if she knew anything about him at all, he had a plan.

All that talk about accomplicing had been a ruse. A tactic to distract her until he could ditch her somewhere she couldn't rat him out.

"RAGE!"

She kicked a tombstone. It shifted in the muck like a loose tooth.

"Careful," von Katzen's low voice came out of the rain. "My garden is not ripe yet."

He stalked into view. His blue eyes fixed her, indifferent to the downpour.

"I see my husband found you suitable attire."

"Yes. Thank you."

"You are getting wet."

He hooked one long-nailed finger. He traced a complex symbol in the air. The droplets around his pale hand froze mid-air. He turned his hand around. He made another complicated gesture. The drops spun round, leaving little silver trails. The trails interwove. He flicked his fingers. A silver-grey umbrella floated across the space between them.

She reached out, tentatively, and took it.

"Thank you."

"Everyone needs shelter and protection."

She wiped her face on the corner of her coat. The rain pitter-patted off the magical bumbershoot.

"Are you a wizard?"

"A witch," von Katzen corrected with crisp precision.

"Same thing."

"No. They are different words and words matter. You know this. Apophax tells me you have many words."

"Do you know where he went?"

"Yes."

"But you're not going to tell me."

Von Katzen sat on a lichen-skinned grave slab. He motioned for her to do the same.

"Shall we play a game of quid pro quo?"

She joined him on the cold granite.

"If we must."

"We must."

He took a deck of over-sized cards from within his cassock. Holding them in his left hand, he opened his right palm. The cards whirled up in an arc over his head. They shuffled themselves. They settled in his open hand. He dealt three, face down, in front of her.

"The truth you put in," he said, "is the truth you get out."

His eyes pinned her to the granite.

"How did you come to be here?"

"I found an old man stuck in my garden hedge and stupidly tried to help. One thing led to another from there."

Von Katzen raised his left index finger. The card to Madarena's left flipped over. A hedgehog played on the back. A long strand of blue thread tangled him up. One foot hovered in the empty air over the edge of a cliff. Entranced with the string, he didn't seem to notice the threat.

"The Fool," von Katzen said, matter-of-factly. "The truth, you chose to quo. Good choice."

"What does it mean? No! Wait! I want to know why he left?" she hastily amended her question.

"The Fool follows his own path. Or hers. Does what no one else will. Maybe there is a reason no one else will. Maybe not. The Fool can't help but play. And off the cliff he goes."

Madarena noticed something on the card. She leaned in close to confirm.

"Look there, though! The blue thread leads off away from the cliff. It might be tied to something so he won't hit bottom. Ha!"

She leaned back, smug. She felt she'd scored a point, though she didn't know what game they were playing.

"It might." He did not sound as if he believed that for a second. "How did you convince Apophax to take you with him?"

She hesitated. She didn't know how much von Katzen knew about Apophax's plans. He didn't *like* the old man. How relevant that was, she couldn't be sure.

On the other hand, having yet again been abandoned, she felt little loyalty.

Back on the first hand, she didn't know what von Katzen was up to. Best to give away as little as possible.

"Standard quid pro quo. I had something he wanted and he couldn't get it back unless he took me with him."

"Well played."

Satisfaction surged in her chest. She already knew the next question she was going to ask. She was quite proud of having worked it out, from multiple alternatives.

"Why does Apophax want to find Mouldywarp—your sister?"

A hint of surprise slipped through the witch's self-composed mask.

"The Fates were right to dress her in potential," he murmured to himself.

"Well? Where's my quid?"

"Oh yes."

The card to her right flipped over. A huge ancient tree filled the scene. A tiny pair of eyes squinted from a shadowy nook in its gnarled roots. Peering close as she could, Madarena made out a hunched woman in a dark brown dress. Her skin was grey, her eyes enormous. She held a shovel in black claws.

"The High Priestess digs where no one dares. Unearths thoughts too deep for words. She knows many ways to many places. Apophax needs her to find his way somewhere by burrowed roads. I don't think he'll like the price."

"That's not very helpful."

"The truth you put in is the truth you get out." He tapped the remaining face-down card. "One more quid pro quo."

"Go."

Unblinking, he watched her like a tiger watching a mouse.

"We know why he chose to go with you. The next logical question: Why did *you* choose to go with *him*?"

The truth you put in...

...careful. You don't know what side he's on.

"Oh, I just like the company. One does get lonely, you know."

The second the words tumbled out, she knew she'd made a mistake. The witch shook his head. His pressed lips parted. The needle-tips of fangs shown between the pale pink lines.

"You were doing so well. Why lie in the last stretch? I guess like follows like."

The Fool and the High Priestess cards melted in the rain, streaking the grave-slab blue.

"No!"

She snatched the middle card. All she caught at a glance was the image of a hooded girl in a purple dress, head bowed, holding a watch over her head. Outlines of similar figures receded from her, into infinity. The card dissolved in the downpour, staining her hand the same deep blue shade.

Von Katzen shimmered into raindrops and was gone.

Once again, she was alone.

22.

"FINE!" she shouted at the indifferent monuments. "JUST FINE!"

She kicked a tombstone until it toppled over.

At least he hadn't taken the umbrella with him. She hunkered under it, fuming. She wasn't about to go inside. She couldn't spend the day politely enduring Kitchen Jack's helpfulness. He was sweet, but she didn't need sweet.

What I need is —

She couldn't finish the sentence. She didn't know what she needed. She didn't know what she wanted either. Her life had, till then, been spent dodging other people's needs and wants — or acquiescing long enough to make them go away.

Now everyone had gone away.

It was just her.

And she didn't even have her dictionary.

Her wrist itched again.

The ink from the cards dyed her skin blue. It also highlighted the length of Destiny Thread, still looped thrice round her arm. She'd come out ahead after all!

"Woot!"

Doubt and fuming fled before her happy dance. She shouted through the downpour.

"I know how to find you! You can't ditch me so easily!"

The Thread trailed off across the fence. She followed it down the street. Left. Right. Left again. Left. A long way straight.

She didn't see much of Charonsferry. Hyperfocused on the Destiny Thread, she didn't even notice the rain stop and the sun blaze off puddles and steaming roofs.

Her boots crunched gravel. She found herself trudging a narrow path cut into a white chalk cliff. A hundred meters below, the sea crashed. Two kilometers down the coast, the glum town nestled in the curve of the bay. A few half-sunk boats bobbed on the glinting waves.

The path wound through a field of large white boulders, patched by black moss. At the summit, an ancient tree spread its branches far over the cliff's edge. Despite the steady sea breeze in her face, the Thread pointed compass-straight up the path.

A gust seized the rain-woven parasol. It nearly lifted her off her feet and over the edge. She wrestled it shut. It had a strap, so she strung it across her back. It had a nice pointy end that would jab Apophax's ribs quite well, when she caught up to him.

As she drew near the giant tree, she heard his voice. The wind carried away his words. She picked her way between the boulders. She peered around the edge of the last rock before a wide plot of churned soil around the tree's gnarled base.

Despite the sun, she shivered when the tree's shadow touched her. Framed against the bright sky, the bare branches were stark and dark as night. Dead ivy vines wove around every limb. They dangled down in looped nooses. The nooses swayed, independent of any wind.

Apophax stood, back to her, about halfway between her hiding place and the base of the tree. He leaned at a jaunty angle on Grimsykill's cane.

Dapper as you please. He must really be conning hard.

"...the need for renumeration. Of course. No one disputes that. And, to be sure, the venture I propose is, as you might well expect from a dream of my means and a witch of your abilities, a profitable one. I am amenable to talk of shares, perhaps even as much as an equal division of the net profit."

Talking to Mouldywarp.

As best she could, without giving up her cover, she tried to spot the witch. She failed.

In his rakish pose, Apophax waited.

There was no reply but the distant sea-roar and susurrus of ivy nooses. Madarena was unsurprised. She didn't know much about witches (having only just met the one) but it seemed very unlikely Mouldywarp would be attracted by a tawdry profit-sharing scheme.

"Very well," Apophax said, after a long spell of silence. "I did not want to have to resort to this, but I am afraid that your recalcitrance leaves me no choice."

Using the sharp tip of the cane, he drew a complex diagram in the rich soil beneath the tree. He filled it with ever-more-intricate interlocked geometrical shapes. Around the edges, he added squiggles of what, she presumed, was some alphabet she did not know.

Producing several half-melted yellow candles from his pockets, he set them up at intersections of the diagram. He waved his hand over them one at a time and they lit. The flames were small, but, in defiance of the wind, burned steady.

He stepped back from the diagram. In a commanding voice, he incanted long words with entirely too many consonants to be plausible. His eyebrows lunged up, almost escaping the confines of his forehead. His fingers waggled with ferocious earnestness.

His voice grew louder and deeper, until, at the peak of his incantation, he threw his hands in the air and cried:

"MOULDYWARP COME FORTH!"

Mouldywarp did not come forth.

The old man drew himself up to his full height. He smoothed non-existent hair over his glistening pate. With effort, he repositioned his great round belly to give himself an imposing chest. He thrust an imperious nose in the air.

"You leave me no choice."

Oh, this is going to be good.

He hurled himself to his knees.

"Please please please please!" He groveled. "I need your help ever so badly and I can't possibly succeed without you. I'll do anything! Please please please!"

He went on in this vein for quite some time. Madarena could not believe the indignities he was willing to subject himself in order to persuade the witch to come out of her tree. She blushed on his behalf.

When he clasped his hands and shook them at the uncaring tree while exclaiming "WHHHYYYY?" she felt so embarrassed she was about to sneak back down the cliffside and leave him to his shame.

As she turned away, he nipped to his feet. Brushing off his knees, he said: "Well, I'm out of ideas. Any suggestions, accomplice?"

She stepped out from behind her rock.

"How long have you known I was here?"

"Immaterial. Irrelevant and ungermane."

"The whole time, huh?"

"Funny thing about thread. It goes two ways."

"So you didn't ditch me?"

"Never. Quid pro quo."

"What now?"

They stood side by side. They considered the towering tree.

"Did you try knocking?" Madarena asked.

"Did I try knocking? Scoff! Do you honestly imagine I would go through all that spectacle had I not first knocked? You're fired."

Confirming her suspicion that he had done no such thing, he continued: "To prove a point, I will knock again."

He rapped the fist-end of Grimsykill's cane on the thick bark.

"There. I knocked. See? Hrmph. Did I kno—"

"—You should keep her close, Apophax," a small, muffled voice interrupted from beneath the roots.

A segment of burl swung upwards. Behind it lay a pitch-black tunnel. Unmuffled, the voice went on.

"She has potential."

23.

A wee mud-crusted shovel heaved out of the hole. Its owner climbed after.

She stood only half Madarena's height. Her greyish-purple skin blended into the grain of the burl wood. She wore a tattered burgundy dress with a brown leather-trimmed coat. The sleeves of the coat were rolled up to her elbows, revealing filthy forearms. Her hands ended in long nails, black with dirt. Her feet were bare and likewise claw-nailed. Her disheveled grey-black hair hung nearly to her waist, topped by an ushanka of dubious fur.

She pushed the hat to the back of her head. Her enormous brown eyes — taking up fully a third of her face — squinted, as though the shadows beneath the tree were bright as blazing noon. Madarena had the uneasy feeling those eyes saw every wrinkle in her brain.

Apophax bowed floridly.

"Mademoiselle Mouldywarp, I presume. You may not remember me. 'Tis been many a turn of the Orrery—"

Not sparing him a glance, Mouldywarp flung a fist up in his direction.

"Devil's darning needle."

She opened her hand. A silver-green dragonfly buzzed from her palm. It circled Apophax's face in a dizzying blur. When it flew away, the old man's lips had been sewed shut with black suture thread.

"Mrph!"

He staggered backwards. He tried to open his mouth by pure force. He whimpered. He set to picking out the stitches, emitting aggrieved sounds.

"That will take him time."

Mouldywarp picked up her shovel. Using its broad blade to shield her eyes, she looked Madarena up and down.

"You. Accomplice. You seem clever. I like clever. Dislike seeming."

"I'm not sure where that leaves us."

"Me neither. So. Both unsure."

"Right."

"Yes."

Apophax's irritated grunts and nasal whiffles punctuated the awkward silence that followed. Mouldywarp jabbed the butt end of her spade at him.

"Why are you traveling with *him*? No! Wait. Bad question. Better question: What does he want with you? No! Terrible question. Wait. Best question: What do you want?"

She cocked her head to the side. She stared at Madarena, as if counting cerebral creases.

Madarena knew what the answer *should* be, if she were like anyone else.

She should want to go home.

She should want to resume normal old life. To sleep each night in a comfortable bed with decorative pillows. To eat the things everyone eats, to see the places everyone sees and say the things everyone says about them. To learn the things everyone knows. To get older at the regular pace and, in due proper course, safely land in von Katzen's garden.

Any ordinary woman who'd been through the past 48 hours of her life would want nothing else.

But.

As her mother had often noted (with the same lip-twist of disdain she used for the word 'individual'), Madarena 'wasn't like other people.'

"I want to know what's going on. What's *really* going on."

Mouldywarp sucked her teeth.

"Ambitious."

"I got nothing better to do."

The witch crooked a dirty claw at her.

"Come with. I promise nothing. You may learn something. You probably won't. That's on you."

She climbed back into the hole beneath the swaying ivy-noose tree. Madarena followed. Apophax, still picking dragonfly sutures out of his angry red lips, lurched after them.

"Mish Moufywahp, thish is mosht impropah. Mish Rua ish my accompwish."

"No."

One of the tree's lower branches bent down. Ivy lassoed Apophax's ankle. The branch sprang back, yoinking him off his feet. He bounced a few times before settling into an angry sway, arms crossed over his chest.

"Shorry." Madarena curtsied. "Ladiesh only."

She squeezed into the tunnel. Convenient handholds took her to the bottom. The burl-hatch closed of its own accord.

"Are you going to teach me magic?" she asked the darkness.

"Don't be stupid. Magic is not something you learn. It's something you do. If that's who you are."

"Ok. Will you teach me who I am? Maybe I'm a woman who can do magic."

"Pfft."

A pale green glow illuminated Mouldywarp's face. She held out her palm. A corpulent phosphorescent grub squirmed in her hand. Madarena took the meager light. She cupped her hand to keep it from wriggling free.

"Thank you."

Without another word, Mouldywarp led Madarena deeper and deeper. Hunched over, she struggled to keep up. Tunnels branched and intersected. In no time, she was quite lost. She wished she could remember the dream trick of walking all the paths at the same time.

Music distracted her from the tunnel to her right. She paused, not noticing Mouldywarp move out of the tiny radius of grub-light.

Dozens of different instruments and voices blended in a complex theme and variations. It was unlike anything she had ever heard—yet she felt sure she'd known the melody from her cradle.

As she listened, lost in the music, she gradually became aware that something was wrong with that symphony and song. A voice was missing. Holes in the harmony. Spaces between the notes. Like worms had eaten the sheet music.

Drawn towards the sound, she took two halting steps towards it. Mouldywarp was there, blocking her path.

"Not there, not yet. Not you." She held her shovel across Madarena's chest. "Back. Back. That way."

Reluctantly, Madarena complied. She tried her best to keep hearing the song. It faded fast. She couldn't keep it in mind.

"Bother," she muttered, trying to revive it. "Ta da ta ta tee da... no... da dum da da doo... imprecation..."

"Quiet. No good to remember. You won't."

The witch spoke true, though it did not stop Madarena from trying, as they burrowed on.

At long last, they came to a door. It swung open. Beyond, the great room of a cozy cabin welcomed them.

"Come in. Toast and tea. Then talk."

24.

While Mouldywarp bustled up refreshment, Madarena stepped into her home.

She ducked at once, reflexively. Not because the ceiling was low. There *was* no ceiling. For a dizzying moment, she thought she would fall right out of the house.

The room lay open beneath a night sky dusted with a smattering of stars. The brightest star shone bright as the moon, though a tenth the size. She didn't recognize any of the constellations.

The full-building skylight wasn't the most disconcerting part of the place.

A pock-marked, dusty, grey landscape spread across the windows. It cut to nothingness at a horizon less than a hundred meters off.

"Where are we?" she asked, breathless from vertigo.

"Pharmakos. Witch's home."

Mouldywarp set a loaded tray on a table by the fireplace. The burning logs in the river-stone hearth did not crackle or smell of smoke.

The whole home struck Madarena as fake—a very convincing facsimile of a mountain cabin. Books lined built-in shelves, changing titles as she watched. Flowers in a window box looked brittle, as if made of shaped glass or encased in lucite.

"This is it? The whole world?"

Mouldywarp clucked. "A piece of it. My piece of it."

"Where's the rest?"

"Here and there." She chanted a little ditty: "Pharmakos undone, scattered far from the light of its sun, in pieces floats in the endless void. The witches who did it, don't regret it, for each one gets her own asteroid."

She poured two tiny cups of tea. "Or his own, I suppose. Is good to be alone, is the point. Witches don't like others. Except my brother. And look where that got him."

"I think," Madarena pulled her swimming gaze from the vanishing horizon, "I need to sit down."

"Then sit. Not fancy here."

Her legs gave out. She thudded to the floor. Mouldywarp dragged a wee stool next to her. She pressed a steaming cup of tea into Madarena's unresisting hands. She patted the girl's arm.

"The world—" the witch started. "No."

She stopped.

"The quaquaverse..."

"The what?"

"Quaquaverse. It's the word for all the worlds that might be. Does not matter. Whatever you call Everything, this is stranger than you thought, yes?"

Madarena held the cup to her face. Breathing the tea fumes cleared her head and settled her churning belly. She nodded.

"Fuller. Bigger. More?"

"Yes."

"And you? With your story?"

"Very, very small."

"Good!" Mouldywarp took a sip of tea. She smacked her lips and made a happy little noise. She brushed a stray worm off her cuff. "We have a start."

"Do we? I feel like I missed the start. Like I came in in the middle and everyone already knows how it ends."

"Maybe. Maybe not. Start, middle, end. Does not matter. Here you are and where you are is here. Far from home. Wearing a dead girl's dress and Potential Coat. Umbrella made of rain slung over your back. Destiny Thread 'round your wrist. Caught in a great complicated Plan like a mouse tangled in a trap. That Plan? Maybe not so big. Not too big for you. Yes."

"I think it might be."

"Pfft! You think." She tapped Madarena on the forehead. "What do *you* know what you think?"

"I used to."

"You thought you did."

"I suppose. I don't know where that leaves me now."

"Here!" Mouldywarp spread her little arms as wide as they would go. Tea slopped over the rim of her cup.

"A story—especially our own—looks so big. What is one story compared to all the stories? Small. Yes."

She pinched a forefinger and thumb tightly together and held them up to her enormous eye.

"And all the stories together, what are they? Smaller than one dot in the 'i' of the word Everything. Yes."

"So I'm basically nothing?"

"Pfft. Everything or nothing. This word or that word."

"Well?"

Mouldywarp segued. "Why did Apophax tie you up with stolen thread? Why you?"

"I think it was an accident. He was just trying to escape the Anubises and found me."

Mouldywarp slammed her cup into her saucer, sending tea everywhere.

"Pfft! That one? Accident? His plans have smaller plans inside them and those plans have even smaller plans."

She snapped a dish towel from the rack. She got on her hands and knees to mop up spilt tea.

"Those plans? Smaller plans, probably. Who can see so small?"

"Not me. All I know is, he's looking for Aoede."

Madarena would've thought it impossible, but Mouldywarp's eyes got even larger. She dropped the sopping towel.

"Kull wahad! After all!"

"Who is she?"

"A Muse, that one. From Mnemosyne. Once. Till she fell in love with a dream."

"Apophax."

"Clever. Quick. I will tell you how this came to be."

"About time."

"Oh yes. It is about Time."

Madarena could hear the capital letter. She held her questions. She was finally getting somewhere and didn't want to miss a word.

"Apophax in those days, young he was. Not so spindly. Not so silly. Not so bald. Charming, even. If you can be charmed."

Kitchen Jack had said the same thing. Madarena still didn't see it.

"This dream, Apophax, he sees a far-off Muse in the world of Mnemosyne. From Oneiros he casts his image to her. They meet. They speak. She sings for him and they fall in love. That part is not much important."

Mouldywarp pursed her lips. Her expression left no doubt how little she thought about a love story.

"There was another dream. Apophax's brother. Kataphax, his name then. Jealous dream. Weak and dull. Boring. Clever—maybe more clever than his brother even. He wants Aoede. Not for love."

"Why then?"

"Power." The witch spat the word like an imprecation. "And for power, Kataphax waits. He baits a trap for Apophax. He convinces his brother to bring his love from Mnemosyne to Oneiros."

"He kidnapped her? Wait—she's a person? Grimsykill and Chironex kept talking about a statue."

"About Time, I said, the story. Muses, they live outside of Time. Maybe each lives in a moment. Maybe they all live in every moment. It does not matter. Put them in Time and they freeze. Like she is now, a little object to put on a shelf."

"Apophax turned her into a statue?!"

"He did not know. He thought he knew. Like you, thinking you know what things mean because you read words in a book."

Madarena flushed. She didn't know whether to be insulted or embarrassed. It was true that her dictionary wouldn't have been as much help here as she might have thought two days earlier. Still, she had to believe it wasn't totally worthless.

"What happened then?"

"Good. Questions. Better than interruptions. Apophax brought her to Oneiros. Much magic stolen to make that happen. A surprise, he thought. For his love. Surprise for both of them. He calls her across the empty space between the Worlds and she appears. One last look and poof!"

Mouldywarp snapped her fingers.

"Frozen. Kataphax pounces. Ha! He laughs. He grabs her. He runs. He uses her power to build himself from a weak and idle dream into the Night Mayor. Powerful. Ruler of Oneiros. Controls many wicked and terrible things. Pays terrors and demons the cruel coins their twisted hearts demand. Spins horrible wishes out of Aeode's imprisoned inspiration."

"What about Apophax?"

"He runs away. Across the quaquaverse. Abandons her. Or so everyone thinks. Now? Maybe not. Plans within plans, that one."

25.

Madarena stared into the darkness between the stars. She said nothing. She didn't know what to think. She didn't know how to feel. It was like every feeling and thought slowly drifted through the vacuum. Pity for Apophax, whom she thought had been a rat. Anger at the Night Mayor. Sorrow for Aoede, frozen in time far away from home.

None of it touched her blank core. She sat far outside the confused orbit of emotions, indifferent as a distant star.

"What am I supposed to do?"

"Read the tea leaves."

That brought her back to Mouldywarp's asteroid cabin.

"Does that really work?"

The witch snorted.

"No. Leaves. Clouds. Guts. Flipping your dictionary and tapping a word and doing what you think the word tells you to do. Tricks for children to fool themselves."

"What about von Katzen's cards? They showed me Apophax. And your tree. And—"

She stopped. She did not know what the hooded girl with the watch meant.

"Such trinkets show you what you would see, if you were there. Or what might be. Potential."

"That word again. Potential. Everyone keeps telling me I have it."

"You wear it on your back."

"This old thing?" She plucked the muslin hoodie sleeve. For a split second there were two of her hands, slightly out of sync. "Hold on! You mean for real, don't you?"

"Potential for real. Now you understand."

"This hoodie—it lets me try things out. Lets me be other versions of me! Like in the maze. I thought that was just a dream."

"Dreamscapes make it easier to see potential, yes."

"Easier? That means I *can* work it elsewhere."

"The Fates gave it to you. It's yours to work wherever."

Madarena didn't bother bringing up that 'gave' wasn't the correct verb. She was too preoccupied, imagining all kinds of uses for the ability.

"Can you teach me?" Hastily, she added: "Quid pro quo, of course."

"I go where I want. I do what I do. What should I want from you?"

"Please? There must be something we can trade."

She riffled her pockets. Planck's watch and von Katzen's umbrella made up the sum total of her possessions. The witch sniffed at both when proffered.

Madarena had never wanted anything so badly as to learn how to harness the Potential Coat. Her head buzzed. Suddenly, a dozen voices talked over one another at the same time, each making a different argument for why Mouldywarp should teach her.

One of them at least must have made the right case, because the little witch chuckled.

"Fine, fine. All of you be still. Settle before you disappear."

Just like that, there was only one Madarena again.

"So you'll do it? You'll teach me?"

"Pfft. You have already begun to teach yourself. Still. I will save you some time. Sit."

Madarena sat cross-legged on the witch's undersized sofa. Mouldywarp picked up a heavy clay jar. It had been shaped to resemble one of the fish-monsters in the Chthonon garden. She set it on the coffee table. She lifted one of the tentacles and the top of the jar flipped open. Madarena leaned over to check out the contents.

"Tush tush! Back. Eyes. Closed."

Madarena complied. She heard a tapping, as of fingernails on ceramic. The smell of fresh-baked cookies filled the air.

"Yes. Your nose. Primal. Hunger. Short-cut through all the thoughts and words that confuse and muddle what you really want. Breathe deep. Now. Open."

Two cookies—one ginger spice and one chocolate chip—sat in Mouldywarp's wee palms.

"Which one? You can only have one. Both are good. So good."

Madarena reached for the steaming spice cookie. She hesitated. Her hand hovered over the chocolate chip. Mouldywarp's big brown eyes watched her impassively.

"Tick tock. If you wait until they cool, you get nothing at all. You must choose. Now!"

The witch's voice barked an order.

Torn, Madarena watched her hands split. They took each cookie. Two versions of her wolfed down one apiece. Somewhere between them, she decided she preferred the ginger spice. Suddenly she held only one cookie. Mouldywarp dropped the other, uneaten, into the fish-monster jar.

"There. You see. Potential."

Madarena nibbled at the cookie. "So I have to really want something? But I wanted both of those cookies."

"No. You wanted the most delicious cookie. You did not know which one was which. Your coat? That gives you the ability to test out Potential. To see without trying."

"I think I understand. Sort of." She brushed crumbs off her lips. "Maybe I need another cookie to practice on."

Mouldywarp chuckled. "No, no. One proves the point. Two would be greedy."

She closed the cookie jar and trundled it back to the counter.

"What if there are more than two options?"

"Same, same. You find what you really want. Center yourself. Don't think, just watch inside." A dirty nail tapped her forehead. "Here. Watch. And when you know what you want, you can see the versions of you that get it. Then you can choose the best. Or not. Your decision."

"Lots of times I don't know what I want. What do I do then?"

"Then? Potential can't help you."

Madarena meditated on that.

"One more thing," Mouldywarp said. Her eyes grew even wider, in deep earnest. "Do not get lost in Potential. Spend too much time on what Might-Be, and you will break apart. Drift. Do nothing but walk roads that never will be, while Doing-What-Is will pass you by."

"How will I know how much is too much thinking?"

"When it is too late."

The grim finality of that perturbed her. Madarena felt sure there had to be a clearer answer than that. Her reflection in the witch's eyes gave no further reply.

She stood up. She shook crumbs from her hoodie.

"Quid pro quo. What do I owe you?"

"Nothing. I teach you because I want. Not everything can be bought."

"A noble sentiment," Apophax said from the doorway. "Don't let anyone hear you. The whole quaquaverse might grind to a halt."

Madarena whirled.

"How did you find us?"

He raised his wrist. "Funny thing about thread. It goes both ways."

"I should've let the Moirai snip it when I had a chance."

"The Night Mayor would doubtless agree. For now, since an invitation is not forthcoming..."

He stepped inside. He poured himself the dregs from the teapot. Tendrils of ivy still clung to his ankles. Mouldywarp closed her door with a chilling *snick*.

"With a witch, you want to trade, Apophax?"

"Times are desperate."

"Not for much longer."

"Hold on," Madarena interrupted. You can't quid pro quo with him. We weren't done yet!"

"Accomplice, if you possess anything worth anything to a witch, I'm over-paying you."

"You're not paying me at all."

"My point exactly. Now, to business." He returned his attention to Mouldywarp. "Since, as you aptly put it, the minutes dwindle, I will be brief."

"I know what you want. I can read the leaves."

Madarena snerked. Apophax ignored her.

"If that is so, then you know I have nothing left to offer. Nothing that will be worth free egress from Logos, at any rate."

"You do not have nothing," Mouldywarp replied. "One thing remains."

Apophax held out a tiny wad of paper. It floated out of his palm. Mouldywarp traced a grey trail through the air. The Plan unfolded. It turned, so Aoede's portrait looked down on them all.

"Kull wahad," the witch whispered again. "Your accomplice told the truth."

"I'm working with her on that," Apophax's sad tone did not match the glib joke.

The three of them stood, transfixed by the picture of the Muse. Madarena heard the melody—it woke within her the memory of the song echoing down Mouldywarp's tunnels. Apophax and Mouldywarp spoke somewhere in the far distance. She barely registered their brief interchange.

"Could I but revive within me, her symphony and song..." Apophax murmured.

"You will steal her?" Mouldywarp said. "The Muse frozen by a Dream?"

"Yes."

"You will go to Logos? Knowing the price the Fates demand?"

"Yes."

"And then? Keep her for yourself? Overthrow the Night Mayor? Take revenge? Hold her in your arms and love her?"

"None of the above. She will be taken home."

"Ah. The accomplice. Plans within plans within atom-sized plans."

"Yes."

"Then I will meet her there. And the witch-road to escape will be hers to walk."

"Done."

"Done."

At Mouldywarp's final word, the cabin around them tumbled down like a stage backdrop. The black sky broke into a billion dusky pieces. Madarena reached out to Aoede's image, still filling all of space. The Muse receded fast as light.

She and Apophax lay once more on the seaside cliff. Mouldywarp's ivy-noose tree was nowhere to be seen.

26.

By the time they reached the outermost shacks of Charonsferry, a glowing snot-colored fog had congealed all round them. Apophax led her down a short mossy stair to the waterfront, away from von Katzen's home.

"Aren't we going to say goodbye?"

"I prefer a quiet exit."

"I'll miss Kitchen Jack."

He surprised her with his wistfulness. "Me too. On we go."

Rot chewed the boardwalk planks, gnawing them away almost in visible time. Wood-worms wriggled underfoot. On her own, Madarena wouldn't have trusted them to carry half her weight. Apophax didn't seem bothered. So she clomped after, trying to match his footsteps.

"Are we not going back through Triskadeka Fair?"

"How would we manage that?"

"I figured you'd stolen von Katzen's passport."

"An obvious plan. I'm insulted."

"Sorry."

"A bagatelle. No, there are more ways to walk the worlds than witches or moonlight stairs. Although—"

He abruptly stopped. She bumped into the back of him.

"OW!"

Even not bristled, his quills pricked.

"It occurs to me we may have difficulty procuring passage. The ferryman can be eccentric in his pricing. And my original accomplice, who would've solved that problem, had a change of heart."

"I had nothing to do with that!"

"I didn't say you did. Until now..."

He leaned in close to scrutinize her by the fog's wretched glow. She practiced her best von Katzen tarot face. With a harumph, he spun on his heel and continued down the pier.

At the end, a wrought-iron sign arced over their heads.

CHARONSFERRY

Beneath that a piece of bleached driftwood dangled on two lengths of chain.

anywhere you can afford
nowhere you want to go

Gobbets of red rust dripped from the iron letters onto the creaking boardwalk. A flat-bottomed scow was tied up to the end of the pier. A tall figure stood at the bow. He held an oar, twice his height.

"Behave yourself and be silent," Apophax whispered. When she opened her mouth to object, he raised one finger. "I mean it. As much as I ever meant anything. This is not a place for flippant wit."

Madarena had not thought him capable of real fear, till just then. She nodded.

"Good."

With a smile a hair too wide and a spring in his step a hair too high, he jaunted down the last few meters of the pier.

"Ahoy! Ferryman!"

The boatman's head turned, slow as decay. Wrinkles creased his face—so deeply, Madarena wondered if they didn't go straight through to the other side. His skin was brittle and yellow as ancient book paper. His mouth collapsed over toothless gums, cracked lips wet with a fine sheen of drool. His eyes sunk so deep into their sockets they were only deep hollows traced by white brows.

Despite his decrepitude, he stood ramrod straight. His arms bulged with thick, ropy muscles. His eyeless gaze fixed on Apophax as the dream approached.

"Charon, I presume?"

He held out a hand. The ferryman did not move. Apophax withdrew the gesture.

"Quite. Hrmph. So. I'll get to tack brasses. Brack tasses. You know what I mean anyway."

Silence. Apophax continued, undaunted.

"As to the matter of the fare..."

Madarena couldn't pay attention to his patter. The vacant pits of the ferryman's eyes absorbed her. His stare filled her vision, eclipsing all else. Apophax's rambling voice, the slap of the water on the pier posts, the hum of undead Charonsferry's night life grew quieter and quieter, as though someone turned down the volume on the world.

She floated in nothingness. A deep and ragged voice surrounded her.

"You... have... time..."

"I suppose. I don't know if we're in a hurry."

The void emanated amusement.

"No..." Charon said. "You... have... time..."

"I don't understand."

"Time..."

Whispering sand slid over itself in an hourglass. A great clatter of grinding gears drowned out the susurrus. That gave way to a *tick tick tick* that yielded to a nigh-inaudible hum that ended in silence.

"I know what time is," she said. "I don't understand what you want."

A grim chuckle filled her head.

"What... do... you... want?"

"People keep asking me that. It keeps changing. Right now I just want to get to Logos. Someplace called Vordem Gesetz."

"With... time... you... may..."

The emptiness snuffled.

"Thirty... seven... seconds... by... the... smell..."

The vivid memory of Planck beneath the Orrery shimmered into view.

The clockwork boy held out his hand. He dangled a tarnished bronze timepiece on a cheap copper chain. It did not tick.

"A broken stopwatch?" She did not recall seeing that in the Plan.

"Thirty-seven seconds. Even Pruftock's been-counters aren't so persnickety. They round losses to the nearest minute."

"Aha!"

She fished the pocket watch out of her hoodie.

"Is this what you want? Quid for going to Logos?"

The dark swallowed up the watch. Charon's ancient voice thrummed in her bones with sonorous finality:

"Done."

Back on the pier, Apophax was full into his pitch. Madarena stood in the scow, on the other side of Charon.

"—naturally there remains the possibility of a future service to be rendered of commensurate value to the transportatory favor which you—I say!"

He waved at her.

"Well done, Miss Rua! You struck the bargain without needing my guidance. Off we go."

He tried to step onto the boat. Charon raised the oar, blocking the path.

"It's alright. I'm with her."

Bluff and guff, he tried once more to weasel past. Effortlessly, Charon swung his oar. The mighty blow knocked Apophax head over heels. The old rogue rolled backwards, off the pier and into the water with a great splash.

The scow's painter line slithered off the cleat. It coiled neatly at the stern. With great beats, Charon drove the boat from the dock. In three strokes, the sickly green lights of Charonsferry vanished. They were at sea.

Anywhere you can afford, the dry mocking voice thought, *nowhere you want to go.*

27.

She huddled in the bow of the scow, hugging her knees for warmth. Flecks of icy water flicked over the gunnels, spitting in her face. The hull planks groaned. Charon's oar slapped the surface and drew back in regular strokes. *Slap shisssshhhh slap shisssshhhh slap shisssshhhh...*

"C-could I have some l-light?" Her voice quavered with the chill.

"No."

Slap shisssshhhh.

"Oh come on, you old ghoul," another voice said, from amidships, "the poor dear is cold and terrified."

"J-just c-cold."

She pulled herself further back into the bow. She wondered how many other people were in the boat—if they even *were* people in the usual sense.

"Well," said the new voice, "let's see what we can do about that."

A spot of light appeared. It brightened. It shone from a large pearl, held in the speaker's left palm. The man—for he was, despite Madarena's fears, a human—sat cross-legged, left leg over right, in the center of the deck. His shaved head was nearly perfectly round. His features, in contrast to Charon's hyperwrinkles, were smooth as a happy baby's.

He wore a simple burgundy robe. A long staff lay cross-wise in his lap. He smiled at her and she could not help but smile back.

The circle of light from his stone grew till she was bathed in it. The light brought gentle warmth and the smell of new grass and peonies.

"Better?

She nodded. "Thank you."

From the stern, Charon grunted.

"Don't mind him," the robed man said. "He doesn't know any better."

Slap shisssshhhh slap shisssshhhh.

Ignoring the gloomy ferryman, the monk put his free hand over his heart. "My name is Jizo."

"I'm Madarena Rua, sir."

She felt like he deserved to be called 'sir'. When he smiled at her again, though, with his wide baby grin, she realized how silly it was to have called him that. She felt stirred up and calm at the same time. It reminded her of how she felt when looking at the sketch of Aoede.

"Forgive me for asking," Jizo said, "but you are early, aren't you?"

"I don't know."

"If you don't know, you are definitely early."

"Better early than late?"

"With words that quick, maybe you're always right on time."

At the sound of his laughter, moans rose over the sea. The cacophony sounded like a thousand lost voices praying in a dozen unknown languages. Madarena shivered, despite the warmth of Jizo's magic pearl.

"Do not be afraid." He rested a hand on his walking staff. "Nothing will harm you while I am here."

"How long will you be here?"

"Too... long..." *Slap shisssshhhh.*

Jizo leaned over. He beckoned her to do the same. He stage-whispered: "He's mad because I'm ruining his act."

Slap shisssshhhh.

"Sorry," Jizo said over his shoulder. "I know you're just trying to break up the monotony." He turned back to Madarena. "A Psychopomp's life is occasionally boring."

"Psychopomp?"

"You might think of us as bus drivers. Or tour guides. Or museum docents, even."

"Ferrymen." Charon growled. "No... need... for... metaphors."

The more he glowered, the more Jizo glowed. Calmly, the monk kept speaking.

"We help people get to and from Thanatos."

"People from where? Just Cosmos?"

"From anywhere, I suppose. Though I haven't traveled every route yet."

"You... will..."

Slap shisssshhhh. The scow slid on over the moaning ocean. Madarena mulled over the word 'psychopomp,' committing it to memory.

"Did you enjoy your visit?" Jizo asked after a while.

"I did!"

"You seem surprised to say that."

"If you'd asked me a week ago whether I wanted to visit a city of the undead to meet a couple witches, I'd call you crazy."

"And now?"

"I'm having the time of my life! I really am. The craziest things keep happening and I'm sure they're all terrible dangerous and not in the least bit good for me and they're all very uncomfortable and every time I think things can't get any crazier or more dangerous or painful, they go and do, and I like it!"

She flailed her arms in consternation.

"It's insane! Why can't I just be bored like everyone else? What's *wrong* with me?"

"Perhaps nothing. Perhaps it always feels good to step into a larger world, even if it also hurts and there is fear."

"What am I going to do next?"

"You should sleep. It's a long journey to Logos. And you may have much to do when you get there."

She curled up. She made a pillow from some coiled rope. She squirmed until she was as comfortable as one can be in the bottom of a boat.

Jizo lowered his pearl. The light dimmed. The warmth remained the same. Charon's steady, hypnotic beat went on. *Slap shisssshhhh slap shisssshhhh slap shisssshhhh.*

Sleep did not come. Her head thrummed. All the events since she'd met Apophax in her parents' garden chased each other around in her brain. She tried to make sense of every incomprehensible thing people had said to her in the past two days, from the Judge in Triskadeka Fair to Jizo's last "perhaps."

Too many loose ends, she fretted, to ever tie off.

She idly fingered the Destiny Thread. The free end strained, taut, over the gunnel. She hoisted herself up for a peek. Like a fishing line, the blue string disappeared into the water, little ripples around its entry.

She glanced over her shoulder. Jizo sat upright and cross-legged, his eyes closed. Charon stared far ahead, not deigning to notice her.

Tentatively, she plucked the Destiny Thread.

It tugged back.

She pulled harder and was nearly yanked out of the boat.

Bracing her feet on the hull, she hauled in the line. Spots swam in front of her eyes. Her forearms burned. Her legs and shoulders quivered, like they might give way any second and send her tumbling into the deadly drink.

A tiny dorsal fin rushed towards her.

"Gotcha!"

One last enormous heave nearly turned her inside out. The catch broke water and slammed into the side of the boat.

The dorsal fin turned out to be an improbably long nose, whiffling quick breaths just above the surface. Grimsykill's cane shot over the hull's edge. A hand hooked the gunnel. Ignoring the quill-pricks, Madarena grabbed the arm.

"Heave-HO!" she shouted.

Apophax surged out of the icy ocean and onto the deck with a mighty: "KaRUMPH!"

Water rained down from his hedgehog coat, spitter-spatting into a growing bilge-puddle.

Thinking quickly, Madarena interposed herself between Apophax and the ferryman. Charon had stopped rowing. He brandished his oar.

"Move."

"No!"

Jizo opened his eyes.

"Ah." His pearl brightened. "This is interesting."

"Move," Charon repeated. "Or... be... moved."

Madarena folded her arms. "No. We had a deal. I gave you time, you can't throw me off. And the only way to throw him off is to throw me off. Quid pro quo."

"Well KARUPHM done my GAHORK accomplice." Still on his hands and knees, Apophax coughed up half an ocean's worth of water.

Jizo stuck his pearl in the air. It stayed there, held by nothing. He stood, graceful as a cat unfolding into a sunbeam.

"Let's have a look at the fellow."

Apophax stood on wobbly legs. "I am sorry. You are not seeing me at my best."

"I cannot help but see you at your best."

"Accomplice?" he muttered in Madarena's ear, "Who is this personage?"

She waved him quiet. Jizo looked him up and down. It was a deep inspection, though the methods and criteria she could not figure out.

"Yes," he said at length. "He will do."

Charon flexed his forearms.

Madarena steeled herself. She took Apophax's hand. She fixed the ferryman with a 'dare you' glare. Jizo simply continued, as though there weren't the tension of immediate violence across the craft.

"You know the law of the Thanaton Sea, Charon. Every passenger gets a psychopomp. Except children, who get two. One to take them the way and one to show them the way."

"You..."

"I deputize this one. He will do well for a stand-in."

By chance, Madarena glanced at Apophax when Jizo said that. The old rascal blushed. Blushed! She scarce could believe it.

He caught her staring. He quickly covered the moment with an unnecessary 'GAFLORK!' and a shake of his sopping coat.

"Fine... you... go...." Charon dropped his oar back in the water. He resumed rowing.

Jizo pressed his hands together. He bowed.

"Madarena Rua. Remember this: Discomfort is inevitable if things are interesting. There is nothing wrong with wanting things to be interesting."

"Do you have to go? I was hoping—"

"Don't hope," he said with a beatific smile. He plucked his magic pearl out of the air. He slung his staff over his shoulder. "Just *do*."

With that, he faded from sight, leaving only the smell of peonies and a faint glow over the whole of the scow.

28.

"Capital!"

Apophax rubbed his hands together. He scanned the craft for a place to rest. He headed for the bow, a safe distance from the sweeping reach of Charon's oar. Soaked, his coat hung limp round his spindly frame. Bereft of the bristling quills, he struck Madarena as small and frail.

His manner, however, was every bit as grandiose. He settled in, as if the scow were a Pharaoh's pleasure barge and he the king of Egypt.

"We're making good time." He paused. "Speaking of time, did I hear right? Did you trade Charon time for passage?"

"I guess. Isn't that what you had Planck steal that thirty-seven seconds for?"

"Not the whole thirty-seven seconds! Much too dear a price for a simple crossing. Did you even *try* to bargain? Ah, accomplice, we need to teach you the value of things before you go and do any further quid pro quoing."

"Oy! It was just thirty-seven seconds."

"Just? Time's the most valuable thing there is, girl. There never is enough of it. You'll see."

"Maybe if you'd told me the Plan in advance, I would've known better. This one's on you."

Ignoring her, Apophax bantered at Charon.

"I say, old boy, whatever are you going to do with your new-found windfall of seconds?"

"Vacation."

"Beg pardon?"

"Go on vacation," Charon unhelpfully elaborated.

"For thirty-seven seconds?" Madarena interjected. "Not much of a trip."

"I'm saving up."

"Good to know..." Apophax muttered under his breath. "For future bargaining."

He set to pulling off his boots. Waterlogged as they were, it proved a difficult task. Madarena ignored his grunts and strains.

"I don't understand," she asked Charon. "Why can't you just take a vacation?"

Slap shisssshhhh.

She repeated the question.

Slap shisssshhhh.

"I don't know how long the trip is, but I can ask the same question for a very long time."

"I can vouch for that," Apophax chimed in, wringing out his socks.

Charon relented. "Until the End of Everything there are people lined up to cross over. So many people. I can't take a vacation. Who else would do my job?"

"I'm sorry."

"Don't be. I collect time. From every passenger who has wasted it, not spent it to its fullest. The dribs and drabs left over. When the End comes and the last person steps out of my boat, I'll use it all up, for a little vacation before Everything's done."

"What will you do?"

"You could try fishing," Apophax helpfully interjected. He whirled his socks in circles to speed up the drying process. "I hear people find that quite relaxing."

Charon's deep grumble echoed from his chest, as if from a bottomless cave.

"Be nice," Madarena said to Apophax.

"I'm still wet. And I've got a terrible pain right here the exact shape of an oar blade. I'm being as nice as that allows."

The ferryman chuckled to himself.

"Are you sure you can't get time off? Who makes you do this? Who's your boss?"

"It doesn't work that way."

"Why not?"

"The line. All those people. They need to cross over."

"Maybe they would find some other way. Maybe they're lined up because they know you'll always take them."

"The boat is slowing," Apophax observed, leaning over the prow.

Charon resumed powerful strokes. "No. It wouldn't do."

"Have you ever tried?"

"No."

"Then how do you know?"

"I know. You are too young to understand."

She'd been told that often enough to know that even though it probably wasn't true (she felt quite sure she *could* understand, given a decent explanation), the person saying it didn't understand the thing themselves. Not understanding it themselves, they used her age as an excuse to avoid explaining it.

She gave up. She rejoined Apophax. He had redonned his socks.

"Don't feel bad," he said, looking into his boot. "You got more words out of him than anyone else in the last three thousand years."

He poured water from the boot over the side.

"That's something, I guess."

He shook out the last few drops. "Don't underestimate it. Your ability to ferret out answers from even the most recalcitrant interlocutor is one of your most useful qualities."

Suspiciously, Madarena thanked him.

"You are sincerely welcome."

He poured out the other boot. He tapped the toe pensively on his cheek.

"I sometimes wonder if the Moirai were mistaken in outfitting you with Potential. Something in Ferret might have been more apropos."

She smoothed down the tatters of the toile hoodie.

"I think they did a decent job. Even if they weren't nice about it."

"The Fates seldom hrrrgh—" He struggled to shove his foot into his boot without rolling overboard.

"Why did you tie the Destiny Thread to me?" she suddenly asked.

Apophax's grip on the boot slipped. It flew across the boat, straight at Charon's head. He moved aside without missing a beat. The boot splashed into the black water.

"Isn't that just the way?" Apophax heaved a resigned sigh. "I found those in the belly of a Chthonon fish-god. Won't be finding another pair like that any time soon."

He tossed the other boot after its brother. He rummaged around inside his voluminous coat. He pulled out a pair of penny loafers, lacking a penny each. He wiggled a finger through a hole in one toe box.

"Disreputable," Madarena said.

"It'll have to do."

"The Thread? It wasn't in the Plan—either the original or the copy you gave me. So why me?"

"If I answer this question to your satisfaction, do you promise to give me peace? It's been a long trip and a weary day and I am much beleaguered."

"Promise. Quid pro quo."

"Very well. Get comfortable."

With a flourish, Apophax fluffed two over-stuffed pillows out of thin air. He shoved one between himself and the bow. He gave the other to Madarena.

She curled up amidships. The pillow cradled her head perfectly. It was cool and comfortable and smelled like new-washed linen. Almost at once, she got drowsy. She did her best to pay attention.

"At the risk of being too philosophical," Apophax started, "let us assume that everyone has a Destiny laid out for them. Whether they can change that and to what extent is not important. At least, not as far as your question is concerned. What matters is that Destiny is a thread handled by the Anakans—like the Moirai.

"Mean girls," Madarena mumbled, shoving her head further into her pillow.

"Quite. They usually travel in packs of three. One to spin the Thread when you're born, another to measure it while you live, and the oldest to snip it when—well, *krrrk.*"

He sliced a finger across his throat.

"I digress..."

"*Krrrk...*" Her eyelids resisted gravity, almost.

"In its raw form, before it is attached to anyone, Destiny Thread has all manner of interesting properties. I managed to acquire—"

"—steal—"

"Says the girl with the pilfered hood pulled down over her eyes."

She meant to acknowledge the point. Instead she yawned.

"Whichever verb you use, I found myself in possession of a short snippet of the stuff. I was not by any means sure what to do with such a windfall. Until I found myself in Cosmos, Anubises hot on my heels."

"So it was random? Chance?"

"I know you're falling asleep, but this is important. Every plan needs room to improvise. Otherwise, you're just a Logon following a script set out by some past version of yourself."

"I'm not falling asleep," she softly lied.

"At any rate, while the cold distracted you, I looped my stray string around your wrist. I knotted the other end to the inside of my sleeve. When you put on my coat, our destinies interwove. That ensured the Anubises—and everyone else—would think you were me, giving me the extra little bit of time I needed to finish up a few things and spring you from Triskadeka Jail."

"Mrrhrrm?"

The boat rocked beneath her. Her thoughts drifted this way and that. She could not collect them into a coherent question.

"Indeed. It seems I tied the knot a smidge tighter than anticipated. And now our fates are tangled up until I can find a way to separate them."

"Snip, snip, snip, snip..." she muzzily mimicked Atropos's scissor-sound.

"I do hope not."

"You're too clever sometimes," she mumbled her last waking thought. "Like with Aoede."

"Go to sleep now," Apophax whispered in a very small, very old, very tired voice.

And so she did.

29.

"I hope you like eggs," Kitchen Jack crowed, "and fresh biscuits!"

"Yum!" Madarena pulled up a stool.

The kobenhold laid a heaped-high breakfast plate in front of her. "And a bit of rice, chicken, and clams for m'love."

"Thank you, dear." Von Katzen nodded towards her food. "Do enjoy before it gets cold."

She needed no more encouragement than that. She dove in, devouring with great snuffling bites.

She was halfway done when a loud knock interrupted her.

"Wonder who that could be?"

Kitchen Jack danced to the door. As he laid a hand on the knob, the whole wall exploded inwards. He rag-dolled across the kitchen. He hit the counters with a sickening squish.

Grimsykill hulked through the wreckage. Snicker-snacking, Chironex crawled after.

"Did you think you were done with us?" he growled.

Shadows wove from the back of Madarena's chair, rooting her in place. Dozens of potential hers thrashed against the bonds. Her muscles seized. She tried to scream and only a wheeze came out. Her eyes pleaded with von Katzen, who kept eating as though nothing were going on.

"Glee! Visitors! Can I get you anything?"

Beaming a vacuous smile, Kitchen Jack hopped on one leg towards the assassins.

Grimsykill punched him in the stomach. Through the stomach. A shower of scraps burst from the kobenhold's back, showering von Katzen. Oblivious, the witch took small civilized bites of mash.

Kitchen Jack toppled to the floor.

"Wuff. Perhaps some tea?"

"Mistress Chironex, will you please dice this idiot into a million bits to shut him up?"

She pounced. In a flurry of vicious slashes, she dismembered Kitchen Jack. Bound to the chair, Madarena could only helplessly watch. Her heart near broke through her sternum bone.

Grimsykill shoved his scarred fist under her chin, forcing her to meet his eyes.

"Consider this a message from the Night Mayor. We are coming for Apophax and anyone who gets in his way is fair game."

It's just a dream.

With every bit of strength she had, Madarena shoved gibbering terror to the bottom of her brain. She centered herself amid the buzz of Potential, the way Mouldywarp had taught her. Somewhere in all those versions of her there existed one who managed to untie the shadow-bonds and step to the side.

So that's who she became.

Grimsykill snarled. "Cute trick."

"Don't call me cute."

She sifted through her possible selves till she found one making the most offensive gesture imaginable. Actualizing that, she woke, leaving the thugs smashing the dream-kitchen in impotent rage.

Slap shisssshhhh slap shisssshhhh slap shisssshhhh...

She sat bolt upright, back in Charon's ferry.

Apophax snuffled. She unslung von Katzen's umbrella and prodded him in the ribs. He did not open his eyes. She jabbed harder. He squidged his eyes tighter shut and blew out his jowls. One more jab, she decided, should do the trick.

"Oh implacable and impudent accomplice, will you not leave me be?"

She pitched her voice for what she hoped were his ears only. No sense in involving Charon.

"Grimsykill and Chironex are coming."

"I assumed as much. A bagatelle. Both of them put together. Maybe even a demibagatelle. Hardly worth losing sleep over."

"They know about Kitchen Jack and von Katzen. We have to at least warn *them*, don't we?"

"Von Katzen is more than a match for anyone — or anything — the Night Mayor can conjure up, I assure you."

She remembered the cards and the way von Katzen had woven an umbrella from the rain.

"I hope you're right."

"Whether I'm right or not, it cannot be changed. And what cannot be changed must not get in the way of what can. Besides," he concluded, snuggling back into his pillow, "why would they waste the calories killing a witch and his husband? We're the ones they want to strew about the landscape in quivering bite-sized chunks."

Charon's sudden chortle was the most disconcerting sound she'd ever heard.

"Come on, old boy! In what way is that helpful? She's already on edge."

"I'm fine."

Her nails prying divots out of the hull undermined that assertion.

"How did they find me? Can they come here? Is it safe to go back to sleep?"

Apophax let loose a nigh-interminable sigh.

"There was a time when a man could doze for whole minutes uninterrupted by the anxieties of importunate youth."

He rolled himself upright.

"I don't know what Jizo saw in me. I'm not cut out to comfort children across the Thanaton Sea."

"I'm neither a child nor in need of comforting."

"I'll not be lured into disputing either point. Let us stipulate at least that you are modestly concerned about the contents of a recent dream."

"Are you sure it was just a dream? Is Kitchen Jack still okay?"

"Yes, yes. He is as happy and moldy as when you left him. Would it help you relax if I explained how dreams work?"

"Probably not."

"Well, it'll have to. It's all I've got."

He produced a brass spyglass. He handed it to her. Madarena wondered how she had missed all the things hidden in his pockets, back when she wore his coat.

She put it to her eye. She scanned the waters. A raft leapt into view, tossing up and down. A man was tied to the mast. From the look of it, the raft was all that was left of a much bigger craft.

"Alright. What am I looking for?"

"Wrong way. Turn it round, accomplice. Turn it round."

She held the large lens up to her eye. A teeny Apophax, far away, waved at her.

"Yes, I've looked through the wrong end of a telescope before. What's that got to do with Grimsykill murdering me in my sleep?"

"If I weren't riding on your dime, I'd overboard you for insolence. It's an analogy. Dreams live in a world called Oneiros. You may remember it from my passport."

"I do."

"In Oneiros, we—"

"—we? So when people call you a dream it's not just a metaphor?"

"Metaphors aren't just metaphors. No. Stop. We're not here to argue like Logons over the definition of every last thing. Yes. Dreams are people too and we come from a world called Oneiros. People from around the quaquaverse can see us when they sleep, as if through the wrong end of a telescope. And we can seek out sleepers on our end too, if we choose."

"I don't like the idea of a bunch of creepy people staring into my brain while I sleep."

"Must you make everything unsavory?"

"You're the one who ogles unconscious people."

"The ogling is mutual!" He overheard his own objection. "I mean, it isn't ogling! No one ogles anyone. It's a legitimate quid pro quo."

"Oh really? What do the dreamers get out of it?"

"I am glad you asked. Unlike you, the Fates have not blessed most of us with wearable Potential. Dreams offer one of the few ways for people to experience What Might Be and learn from it."

"What about imagination?"

"If only. In time, you'll learn that real imagination is almost as rare as a free Potential Coat."

"Bleak."

"To return to the subject at hand. Grimsykill and Chironex, being dreams like myself, must have spent some time to find your dreamscope and give you a good scare. However, they can no more hurt you there than you could hurt me through the wrong end of a spyglass."

He took it back from her.

"Nor can they step through it. Despite many a love song across many a world, no one actually steps out of dreams."

As always with Apophax, Madarena wasn't sure any of that was true.

"What can I do to keep them from hassling me all night?"

"Hide under an umbrella."

With that, he threw himself back on his pillow. He snored within seconds. She almost jabbed him again for being infuriating. The dim light in the scow made his face look so creased and worn and helpless, she stayed her hand.

"Ok. Umbrella. Why not?"

She opened von Katzen's bumbershoot. It covered her and the pillow nicely, if she curled up in a ball. So she did.

To her surprise—or rather *not* to her surprise, because she was so sound asleep that surprise couldn't enter into it—she fell sound asleep and stayed that way the rest of the trip.

30.

When she woke, grey haze filled her sight. Not the fog of Thanatos—a pall *inside* her eyes, as if cataracts had grown overnight.

She fumbled to feel the deck planks beneath her. Charon's oar had stopped its steady beat. The smell of the ocean was gone. Instead, a cacophony of exhaust fumes, moldering garbage, halitosis, perfumes cheap and dear—a dozen urban odors—filled the air. All round she heard whirrs, hums, screeches, hisses, clatters, rings, millions of babbling conversations.

She rubbed her eyes. Still grey.

"Apophax! I'm blind!"

"Don't be so melodramatic. Put these on and let's go. I want to spend as little of my dwindling time here as possible."

A pair of glasses pressed into her hands. She put them on.

"Kull wahad!" she quoted Mouldywarp.

The scene burst with every color of the rainbow. Every color *between* the colors of the rainbow. More colors on top of that.

At first, the sudden onslaught of color dazzled her too much to make anything out. Gradually, her eyes adjusted to the eight-faceted glasses. She gasped at the riot of sights they showed.

Moving walkways—each wide as the widest highway on Earth—ran all around her, above and below, at every angle, all the way to the horizon. Millions of eight-limbed Logons thronged on them.

"They're all my size! Or am I their size?"

"Same thing," Apophax curtly replied, his lips set in a grim line.

Every walkway was divided into seven lanes; each lane rolled at a different speed. The slowest, a red lane all the way to the right, moved barely faster than a brisk walk. The fastest, the violet lane on the far left, tore along at incredible pace, blurring the commuters riding it.

The conveyor belts stretched between vast glass-and-steel cubes. Lights from their windows glinted off one another, illuminating the whole city bright as day, though there was no sun. The skyscrapers hovered mid-air. Leaning over the edge of the boat, Madarena saw buildings recede below them as well.

"Vordem Gesetz," Apophax leapt from the scow onto a gleaming steel pier. "Hop hop. Mustn't keep Mouldywarp waiting."

Madarena slung her umbrella over her back. She climbed out of the ferry.

"Thank you, Charon. I hope you have a nice vacation."

"Be seeing you."

He pushed off the dock. In no time at all, Madarena lost sight of him amid the criss-cross of conveyor belts and glare of buildings. Still entranced by the multitude of colors, she thought of the stacks of grey paper back in the Strandhome.

"Is this what Logons see all the time?"

Apophax herded her down the dock with little nudges.

"Yes, yes. They are attuned to nuance."

She marveled. She would never have thought pedantic shell-bugs capable of splendor.

Apophax stopped at the step-on point to the nearest walkway.

"Take care now, accomplice. There's a trick to this. Keep up at all costs. I don't want to lose you. Who knows what might happen if you were left at liberty in Logos."

"Chaos, probably."

He took her by the hand. "Inevitably. Now!"

They stepped together onto the red lane. Madarena swayed a little at the sudden acceleration. The pier receded behind them. Apophax released her hand. He sped up as he moved forward, until he matched the pace of the orange lane.

"To the fast lane!" he shouted.

He hopped nimbly over. He shot forward. In moments he was far ahead of her.

"KEEP PACE!"

She ran and jumped over. He'd already gotten up to yellow speed. By the time she caught up, he roared ahead on the green lane.

"QUICKER QUICKER!"

Confident she'd master the trick, she stepped left. She did not lift her right foot—still on the slower, yellow lane—fast enough.

"Yerk!" She spun round. She tumbled over. She rolled down the green road, picking up several bruises.

Luckily, she crashed into another commuter. This stopped her from flying off to her doom. The Logon picked her up. He brushed her off with six arms.

"The roadways are for standing or walking at a reasonable pace only. Most certainly not for tumbling."

"Sorry."

"Don't apologize to *me*. It's the Law."

Apophax had already reached the blue lane.

"Gotta run!"

"No running!" the Logon futilely enjoined.

She caught him on the violet lane.

"WHERE ARE WE GOING?" she shouted. The wild wind carried her words far away. Apophax's lips moved to similar effect.

He tapped his ear. He raised one spindly finger. He rummaged through his pockets. He took out a small wire hoop and a container of sudsy liquid. He dipped the hoop in the suds. He pursed his lips. He blew a long breath. A bubble large enough to hold the two of them hung from the hoop. He stepped inside and she did the same.

The howling traffic wind dulled to a hum. The iridescent soap bubble held firm.

"At some point you realize I'm going to ask about this," Madarena said.

"Chthonic soap is exceedingly sturdy. Has to be, to scrub some of those abominations clean."

She made a mental note to return to the topic later. Her list of topical revisitations had grown quite long by this point in her acquaintance with Apophax.

"Where are we going?"

His eyebrows bristled ominously.

"Oh, accomplice mine, we are going to one of the most dreadful, demoralizing, depressing, depraved, desponding dungeons in the whole of existence."

"The belly of one of those Chthonowatsits fish monsters?"

"Worse."

"A hell world where it turns out all the devils are real and they torture outsiders they catch forever and ever with jabby hot pokers?"

"Wor—wait! That's not even a real world. What a nasty baroque imagination you have, child! Who's been teaching you?"

"I'm an autodidact. Now are you going to tell me what horrifying destination awaits or am I going to keep making things up?"

Apophax squared his shoulders. He stiffened his lips. He gazed bravely into the distance.

"We, my grim and naive accomplice, are going to a bureaucrat's office."

The bubble popped. The howl of the commuter road bore them towards doom.

31.

They arrived late in the afternoon. They stepped off the red lane onto a wide plaza, decorated with fountains and statues of Logons of presumed import. At the other end, a skyscraper flared with blood-red dusk.

Apophax shuddered. "Has it really come to this?"

"'What can't be changed must not get in the way of what can.'"

"That *would* be the one piece of my advice you bothered listening to."

"Come on." She started off at a brisk pace.

All at once, every door to the building burst open. A surge of Logons flooded the plaza. They jostled Madarena and Apophax every which way. For a full fifteen minutes, they treaded crowd to keep from being washed back onto the walkway.

Then, swift as they'd appeared, the Logons cleared out, riding the walkways home in droves.

"Ah, rush hour," Apophax said.

"At least we'll have the place to ourselves."

"I admire your optimism."

A sign spanned the entire second story of the building.

Interworld Property Impoundment and Return, Oneiros & Mnemosyne Division

AUTHORIZED PERSONS ONLY

UNDER PAIN OF LAW

A doorman stood by the nearest entry. He was by far the biggest Logon Madarena had ever seen. Six arms bulged with muscle under a voluminous greatcoat. On his lapel he wore a gold badge twice the size of her head. His eight-eyed glare was so ferocious, she skidded to a halt.

"We're low on time, accomplice. Hop to."

"How are we going to get past?"

"Him? Don't worry about him. True, he could hie us off to an eternity of imprisonment if he thought we weren't supposed to be here—"

"—which we *aren't*."

"A fact of which he is, thankfully, unaware. So stop saying it and walk like you belong."

Apophax demonstrated. She imitated.

"No, no. Like you *belong*. You've developed a skulking slouch in the short time I've known you."

"Comes of keeping bad company."

"I'll telling Mouldywarp you said that."

"Devil's darning needle."

And, just like that, they were in the airy marble-floored lobby. Apophax's 'we belong here' strut worked. The guard had even held the door open for them.

Madarena could think of all kind of future uses for that swagger. Some even not illicit.

Apophax hunched over a terminal labeled DIRECTORY. He pecked at the screen with agonizing slowness. By the fourth laboriously selected menu poke, Madarena couldn't stand it. She hip-checked him out of the way.

"Here."

"We are searching for—"

"K. Landvermesser, yes, yes." She focused on navigating the directory. "Assistant Undersecretary, Interworld Property Impoundment and Return, Oneiros & Mnemosyne Division."

"How did you—?"

"—Tsk! The card in your pocket. I pay attention. Now let your accomplice do her accompling. Accomplification? Accomplicize?"

"Less lexicon, more lookicon."

"Not a word." Multitasking only slowed her a tick. She brought up the Assistant Undersecretary's information. "23rd floor, Office 217."

"You may want to take the stairs." Apophax's voice dropped to a strained whisper.

A large bank of elevators dominated the center of the lobby. There, positioned in the sunset shadows so no one could pass unnoticed, lurked Grimsykill and Chironex. Their heads swiveled.

"Quicker than I expected," Apophax murmured without moving his lips. He pressed something into her hand. He rolled his shoulders back.

"What are you doing? Let's get out of here."

"Stairwell to your left. Through that door."

Chironex chittered. Grimsykill flexed his murderous paws. There was no way Madarena would make it out of the lobby before they pounced.

"I must be very fond of you," Apophax said. "Because you know how fond I am of me. Now go."

She heard Mouldywarp's voice, echoing from memory. *You would go to Logos? Knowing the price the Fates demand?*

"No!" Her shout broke across the marble vaults.

She seized his arm to stop him from rushing to the fray. His hedgehog quills pierced her hand. Screaming in pain, she recoiled.

Apophax jumped forward. He brandished the cane in a fencing pose. His bellow roared fierce and desperate across the hall.

"HAVE AT THEE!"

The Night Mayor's assassins charged.

Blind with fear, Madarena bolted to the stairwell.

Apophax sprinted into danger. Closing on the thugs, he tucked into a ball. Quills bristling, he rolled across the lobby. He crashed into them at terrific speed.

She did not see what happened next. The heavy steel door closed behind her. It was not thick enough to block the thuds and grunts and howls of a desperate brawl to the death just on the other side.

She fled.

She jumped the stairs two and three at a time. Tears burned her eyes. She could not see where she was going, except up. Her chest heaved with sobs and gasps for air. Even when she couldn't hear the sounds of Apophax's last fight, a dozen floors below, they still filled her brain.

She ran until she ran out of stairs. At the very top, a ladder was bolted to the wall. She climbed it and shoved the hatch at the top. By some miracle, it was unlocked. She pulled herself through, onto the roof. Her legs churned on, until she reached the very edge.

Dusk blazed across the glorious rainbow city. She fell to her haunches. Her back pressed the gritty parapet.

No.

Her hand trembled as she lifted her wrist.

A sad frayed end of blue thread drifted in the breeze.

No. No.

She touched it. Snapped clean through.

She snatched the Logon glasses off her head. She did not want to see any more.

No no no no no.

Why?

Apophax, why did you do that? We could've both run.

Stupid stupid.

What am I supposed to do now?

I finally didn't want to be alone and now I'm alone.

Apophax.

Aoede.

At the memory of the Muse, a melody rose from the heart of her sadness. A single stringed instrument played a simple song so sorrowful it turned her inside out. She wept and wept until she was sure she would never, could never, cry again.

The song ended.

Only silence and the distant hum of life in Logos, whirling indifferently on.

And then determination.

Resolve.

She scrubbed her eyes with her raggedy Potential sleeve. She wiped the tears and snot and spit from her face. She put the Logon glasses back on.

I will finish this.

She opened her hand, to see what Apophax had given her before running to his death.

The Plan. She unfolded it. There were only two pieces left—retrieve Aoede from Landvermesser's office and return her to Mnemosyne. Apophax had himself doing both of those things alone. Now —

She stuffed down another round of weeping.

No. Later.

She stood. She glared at the World of Law.

She'd been wrong before. She was not alone. She had herself. She had all the selves she might ever be.

She was strong.

She was fierce.

She was smart and wild and exploding with Potential.

She opened the hatchway and descended into bureaucracy and death.

32.

Grimsykill's voice echoed up the stairwell.

"It's not in his coat, sir."

An officious voice replied: "Then it must be with the girl. Find her."

That's the Night Mayor? He sounds like a hall monitor had a baby with a bowl of plain oatmeal and they named it Fussy Blandpants.

That baby killed Apophax. Keep moving.

Right.

"When you do," the tepid voice continued, "remember she is irrelevant. All that matters is my property."

The first-floor door boomed shut.

Grimsykill's boots clomped upwards, accompanied by the scrape of Chironex's chitinous claws. After a moment, what Madarena presumed was the door to the second floor opened and shut.

They're doing a sweep. They don't know about Landvermesser.

She resisted the urge to run down every path at once. Best to conserve her Potential for when it was most needed. Instead, she stepped as quick and quiet as she could down one flight.

The second floor door opened again and the assassins resumed their upward progress. Madarena froze till they'd moved on to the third floor. She checked the number she was on. 49. She could get to 23 before they would, albeit without much time to spare.

Office 217 proved easy enough to find. As obnoxious as Logons were, their persnickety insistence on organizing and labeling everything did have its advantages.

Unfortunately, they were the kind of people who locked every office, even inside a well-guarded building. Stymied, Madarena shoved at the frosted-glass door.

The press of time squeezed her chest. Grimsykill and Chironex couldn't be more than three floors away. She could almost feel Chironex's razors stabbing her side.

Ow! Hold on...

The stab in her side came from Apophax's lockpicks, which she had tucked away a lifetime ago on Thanatos.

Yes!

No more seconds to waste. She couldn't afford trying five times to unlock Landvermesser's office. She centered herself on what she really, really wanted, the way Mouldywarp had taught her. She pictured all the Madarenas, trying to get past the door. Amid that blur, she found one who nailed the lockpicks on the first try.

Click.

Pride surged. She wished Apophax were there to see.

No. Not yet.

She stifled the wish until she was done with the heist. She could fall apart then, not a moment before.

Inside the office, two beige filing cabinets flanked the door. An inspirational art print, mass-produced and uncompelling, hung on the acoustic-tile wall behind a neatly arranged desk. She passed all of that over, drawn to the sturdy steel safe. Someone had helpfully labeled it IMPOUNDS.

She contemplated the numbered keypad.

She was not a safe cracker.

Nor, after a cursory survey, were any of the possible versions of her that existed. At least, at that point in her life. She added 'safe cracker' to the list of possible occupations she should explore.

You'll be cracked wider than a safe if you don't hurry.

She jabbed at the keys randomly. Within three failed tries, an alarm went off.

The guards arrived surprisingly quickly. They apprehended her before she even got off the elevator. Judgment was swift. The sentence was very, very long. By the time she got out, she was too old to do much more than sit by the window and wander in memories of what might have been.

The next potential future worked out more or less the same. And the next and the next. Her head blurred with failed ends. Hundreds. Thousands. Tens of thousands. She could no longer track them all, the relentless days in prison, the ages of bland grey shuffling towards Charon's waiting ferry.

There were so many nigh-identical Madarenas who couldn't open the safe, they seemed more real than the present her, hunkered in front of the safe.

She only needed one success.

There had to be at least one success. Before she lost herself forever in a haze of Maybe.

And then.

A million failed punch codes collapsed. Dizzy with the effort, she scarce registered the green light, the buzz, and the silent swing open of the thick steel door.

There were a half dozen items in the Impound Safe. Only one mattered. With careful, reverent hands, Madarena lifted the statue of Aoede free.

"Let's find Mouldywarp."

"Let's not," Grimsykill said from the doorway, "and say we killed."

Snick-snack.

She turned to face the assassins. Grimsykill had recovered his brutal cane from Apophax. Chironex's mantis blades flashed in the fluorescent light. Madarena set the statue on top of the safe. She unslung von Katzen's frail, delicate umbrella, woven from rain.

"Alright," she said. "Have at thee."

With a single blow, Grimsykill smashed the desk into a million splinters. "That's what your boss said."

"And it did him as much good as it will do you," Chironex hissed. *Snick-snack.*

Keeping possibilities in her peripheral vision, Madarena stood her ground. Grimsykill stepped within reach.

"Pity. I was hoping you'd run. It's less fun to kill a little girl frozen in fear."

"Needs must, when the Night Mayor drives."

"Very true, Mistress mine. Let's end this."

He raised his cane in both hands. He brought it down fast and hard.

Fwoop.

Madarena opened the umbrella. Her plan had been to step aside so the blow just missed, snatch up Aoede, and run for it. She frantically scanned for the version of her who did that. Too late. The heavy iron fist hit the translucent canopy. She winced in anticipation of pain and death.

Instead, the instant the cane touched the umbrella it exploded into gobbets of rust. A decade's worth of steady, patient corrosion by the rain occurred in a nanosecond. Carried by the momentum of a now-disintegrated bludgeon, Grimsykill hit the floor face-first. He bellowed. He clawed at his eyes, covered in clumps of blood-red decay.

"Imprecation!" uttered a hundred Madarenas becoming one.

She seized Aoede. Planting one boot firmly on Grimsykill's head, she launched herself towards the door.

Chironex's claws tore a jagged gash in the umbrella. She screamed a hideous high-pitched buzz that shattered the tube-lights. In the afterglow, Madarena saw the assassin's forearms wither away from the flapping rain-woven fabric.

Thinking a hard and hearty thanks to von Katzen for his gift, she sprinted down the hall.

33.

The first thing she saw when she reached the lobby was Apophax's coat, crumpled on the floor. She did not have time to mourn. The second thing she saw was the Night Mayor, standing between her and the way out.

She'd imagined him differently.

He looked nothing like his quirky, improbable brother Apophax—no ridiculous limbs, no enormous pot belly. He even had a full head of hair, slicked and parted on the left.

Nor did he appear like the kind of monster she'd have thought necessary to keep Grimsykill and Chironex in line. No fangs nor claws nor blood-red eyes nor muscles rippling to tear and rend.

A dark grey wool suit hung flaccid off his doughy frame. Sallow, droopy jowls defined his querulous pout of a mouth. He stooped under a dowager's hump. His watery eyes bleared at her.

"Madarena Rua." He said her name like a teacher who'd long since given up on everything except attendance.

"Don't get in my way, Kataphax."

He stepped aside. One spotted hand waved to the nearest door.

"I wouldn't dream of it. It seems Grimsykill was right to fear you."

"*He* was afraid of *me*?"

"The fearsome are often, I have found, the most fearful. Doing terrible things has a way of warping one's perspective."

"You would know."

She heard the faint sound of a stairwell door slamming, 23 flights up. She paced carefully towards the door. She held the torn umbrella as a shield. She didn't believe for a second that the Night Mayor was as weak as he seemed, nor that he would just let her walk away.

"Before you go, there is the matter of my property."

"A Muse is no one's property."

"Let's not quibble like Logons. There is a chance here for quid pro quo."

"I don't want anything from you."

He nudged Apophax's crumpled coat with his foot.

"Neither did he."

"You'll pay for that."

"See? You do understand how the world works. So. What will it be? Want me to order Grimsykill and Chironex to be punished? Killed? They did get out of hand. Fine people, but overzealous. I am peaceful myself and never wanted this to happen."

She counted the seconds in her head. The thugs must be somewhere around the 10th floor. She was halfway to the door. The Logon guard watched across the floodlit plaza. He had seen nothing behind him.

"They only did it because you told them to."

"Did I? I recall only wanting back what was stolen. If good people got so angry about the theft that they took matters into their own hands, that is sad, yes. But shouldn't he have thought of that before stealing from me?"

The umbrella shook with impotent rage. She wanted to beat him for his lies. She wanted to smash Grimsykill and Chironex to powder.

But that wouldn't help Aoede. She kept cautiously moving to the exit.

"I understand. You are angry. I am angry too. None of this is fair. Let's make things right with a deal we both can live with."

A shadow fell over them both. An enormous tree suddenly filled the plaza, blocking the bright white floods.

"Some things," Madarena closed the umbrella, "cannot be bought."

She flipped it. She grabbed the tip. She juked towards the Night Mayor. He recoiled, covering his face and wailing. Using the hook handle of the umbrella, she snagged Apophax's coat. She hit through the door at a full run just as Grimsykill and Chironex burst into the lobby.

"This isn't over!" the Night Mayor cried.

Her hands were too full for an adequate gestural reply.

34.

Juggling Aoede, the umbrella, and Apophax's coat, Madarena plucked a stray glow-grub off the dirt wall. Mouldywarp's enormous eyes reflected twin dots of green. Sadness passed across them when the witch saw the empty coat.

"It was always about Time," she softly said. "I guess his ran out."

Madarena did not trust herself to answer without crying. She held up the Muse statue. Mouldywarp nodded.

"Good. Nearly done. This way."

More subterranean tunnels followed. The smell of earth and worms and life growing calmed her breath. Her heart settled into a low cadence. Her muscles let go their vigilant grip on her bones.

"We have to go to—"

"—I know. Shush. Listen."

The faintest wisps of melody drifted from the dark. Mouldywarp led her on. As the music grew, her feet took charge. She no longer needed the witch's guidance. Alone, she reached a singing portal.

The statue in her hands reached out deep brown arms. The cool ceramic warmed beneath her touch. Aoede disappeared.

Beyond the opening lay an impossibly lovely landscape. Vast peaks and bright meadows and crystalline rivers near blinded her. Shielding her eyes, she trotted down a path of alabaster pebbles.

Ahead, Aoede waited, restored.

Behind the damsel with the dulcimer ranged three dozen more Muses, men and women, holding instruments. They glowed in the sun. Aoede smiled at her. The rescued Muse tapped a rhythm with her foot and struck the first few notes of a new and glorious song.

One by one the others joined in. The symphony rose around them. Solid sound lifted Madarena off the ground. She soared over Mnemosyne. Her eyes fluttered shut of their own accord. She lost all sense of time and place, self and other, motion and stillness.

Everything stopped and everything was well.

35.

If she had known how, she would have stayed forever amid the melodies of Mnemosyne.

She did not.

So, she squirmed and shifted on hard, cold, uncomfortable ground. Icy wetness seeped through her hoodie and Kitchen Jack's dead-girl dress.

"Feh. Fine, I'll get up."

The world around her fractured into many tiny identical scenes. She remembered she still wore Logon glasses. Taking them off and stowing them, she looked around. The house and garden around her had an uncanny look.

"Where am I now?"

"You do not know it?" Mouldywarp said from behind her. "You are home."

"Home?"

The word felt like it needed looking up.

"Yes. New now, the old place. Because you are new. Not a girl who needs the dictionary to know what things mean anymore, no?"

"No."

She hesitated.

"What do I do now?"

Mouldywarp and her ivy-noosed tree had already gone away. Madarena was alone again. Still, she did not return to her parents' house.

The windows shone with warm homely light. It was dinner time within. Her mother and father waited at the dining room table. A girl in neat and fashionable clothes bounced into the room. She kissed each parent in turn and took her seat. She chatted away with them, happy as could be.

"Wait, is that me? How is that me?"

"Well, remember when I excised that bit of your shadow back in the Fair?" a muffled voice came from inside Apophax's coat.

Stunned, she dropped it. The tiniest ant-sized dream crawled out of the breast pocket. He balanced on the end of a quill. He squinted up at Madarena, who towered over him.

"This disadvantage won't do. At all."

By the time he'd rolled back to Apophax-size on the other end of his shadow, she was there to tackle him with a wild woot of joy.

"Oof! Careful now, accomplice! I may not be ceramic but I'm still not indelicate. And a modicum of quiet perhaps."

She let him stand. So as not to alert the family inside, she restrained her voice.

"How?"

"Could you be a bit more specific?" He buffed his nails on his lapel with infuriating casualness.

She burbled a bunch of syllables that weren't words.

"Ah. Of course. How did I do all of it? It's really quite impressive. As far as the docile adolescent within, I deemed that necessary. Once I decided to throw you under the Anubis, I realized that absconding with one of the locals while I was in the midst of fleeing from the law myself would be most imprudent."

"Imp—!" was all she could manage before returning to burbles.

"Distracted as you were by my comical appearance and delightsome manner, it proved no difficulty to cut out a bit of your shadow. Then I simply inflated her and told her she was a well-behaved girl who wanted her parents to be happy."

"And you thought that would fool them?"

"We'd only just met."

"Fair point."

"Besides, they seem too relieved to question your sudden change in personality. Everyone's happy."

"Hold on! You're dead!"

She held up her wrist. The slack end of the severed Destiny Thread shimmered in the waning moon.

Apophax bowed his head piously.

"The Fates needed a thread to cut. I gave them one."

He pointed at the quill-coat. She picked it up. The seams frayed. It was already falling apart. It wouldn't last another wearing.

"A shame. I really liked that coat. But, I guess all good things come to an end..."

"Apparently not," she said. "At least now I can do this."

She dropped the coat. She seized him in a hug. She squeezed him till he squeaked. She released him. He dashed a bit of water from the corner of his eye. He smoothed his suit.

"Hrm. Yes. It seems our business is concluded then. You restored my love to where she belonged. The memory of her will have to suffice. You've made it home. All the quids have been quo'd."

Wind rose. Dead leaves scuttled across the snow. Twigs scratched the windows, sending a *scree scree* across the empty night. Madarena remembered Chironex's scythes and Grimsykill's fists.

"The Night Mayor is still out there. He'll be very angry with you. And me."

"I'm afraid so. However, for a while at least he'll be trying to salvage the ruins of his empire, in the absence of a Muse."

"Right! Without Aoede, he doesn't have power."

"True. However, lots of people *believe* he has power. Which is as good as the real thing. Better in some ways. Easier to maintain."

"What will you do?"

"I have a Plan."

"I figured."

"As for you, you needn't worry. Here on Cosmos you're safe. It's time for us to part. Don't worry about your shadow-doppelganger. She'll vanish once you poke her with that brolly. I'd wait till no one was around before you jab her."

"Killjoy."

"It's your choice. For now, adieu, adieu. Dream other dreams and new."

"One last hug?"

"Since it will be the last, yes. I wouldn't want this kind of maudlin display to be a habit."

After one perfunctory, avuncular embrace, he spun on his heel. He took one step toward the hedge. He halted. He strained to move forward.

"I seem," he said, turning, "to be impeded."

"Truly? How impertinent of me."

She lifted her wrist. A thin blue line ran from her arm to the old dream's spindly wrist. His rueful, bested laugh warmed the winter night.

"Oh most impudent accomplice..."

"If you think for all the minutes in Chronos I'm going back to my old life, you're as mad as a fish-monster's mother. We're in this together now. Show me the quaquaverse and maybe I'll let you go. Quid pro quo."

"Where do you want to start?"

She hummed with Potential.

"Anywhere. Everywhere. I'm not sure. When we get there, I'll let you know."

About the Writer

Jake Burnett grew up on four continents and now lives in North Carolina with his wife, a one-eyed cat, and two very wiggly dogs. His first novel, *The Chaos Court*, was one of *Kirkus Reviews* Best Books of 2020.

1. The Offaltosser

The day Patience Fell turned twelve, she bid farewell to her family farm.

Her father gave her a firm handshake. "Be kind," he said.

Her mother gave her a brand-new broom. "Work hard."

Her seven brothers and sisters gave her one hug each.

"You'll do fine," her parents said together after the hugging was done. Without further ado, Patience shouldered her little pack, hopped on the back of a turnip wagon, and turned her face to the road.

The Fells were a country family and not given to displays.

She arrived in the town of Whosebourne early the next morning. Her goal was to find her place in the world. Everyone said that was what you did when you turned twelve, and her parents' farm (with all those mouths to feed) didn't have enough room for her.

The wagon driver let her off at the gate market. In return for the ride, she helped him unload the turnips.

"You sure you know what you're doing from here?" he asked when they were done. "Whosebourne's mighty big."

"Yes, sir."

"Fancy houses sometimes put out signs for broom-girls." He climbed back onto his wagon with a grunt. He clucked the old horse into a slow plod. "Inns too. Look for those."

Patience knew that. It had been her plan all along to find just such a place, but she thanked him for the advice anyway. Gripping her broom, she strode off down the street on her mission.

The townsfolk bustled all around her. They jostled past with very serious faces. No one paid Patience much mind—but then, they didn't pay each other much mind either.

Everyone talked all at once, as if everyone else were listening just to them. Iron wheels rattled on the cobblestone streets. Bells rang over the rooftops. A dozen sounds she couldn't identify echoed from every corner. The combined clatter and chatter of Whosebourne made as little sense as the juts and twits of nervous birds in the dark woods back home.

She was passing an inn called *The Crock and Dice* when she heard a muffled voice under the racket. Someone was crying. Patience stopped. The crowd tried to shove her out of its way. She stood her ground, listening to find the source of the sound.

In the alley next to the inn, a girl about her own age slumped all alone on the stoop of a kitchen door. She sobbed into her apron. A bundle of clothes tied to the end of a broom was propped up against the wall next to her.

No one in the street went to check on the girl weeping in the alley. No one even spared her a glance. So Patience pushed against the flow of uncaring townsfolk, till she cleared the crowd and stood by the stoop.

"Do you need help?"

The other girl replied with jagged sobs. Patience put a hand on her shuddering shoulder.

"AH!" The girl jerked her head up. Her eyes were wide as a spooked stallion's. She wasn't looking at Patience though.

Leaning out of the garret window of the inn, three stories up, a woman with ink stains on both cheeks was watching them. She cocked her head to the side. She whistled a curious three-note tune.

"Tu-whit, tu-whoo!" she chirped.

"No!" the girl on the stoop shouted up. "You're all mad and I won't fix it!"

Just then, the wind rose in the alley. A scrap of fish-stained butcher paper danced across the cobblestones. Several more bits of garbage whirled around Patience's feet.

"Offaltosser!" The girl leapt off the stoop. She seized her broom-and-bindle. She sprinted into the street, muscled through the crowd, and disappeared from view.

That's when things took a turn for the odd.

The bits and scraps and snips of trash blowing around the alley swirled up into a funnel cloud of mess. This whirling thing hovered in front of Patience, twice her height.

"Fox in a bonnet!" she cried. (It was something her mother said when surprised.)

She swiped with her broom at the tumbling pieces of garbage. The funnel jumped back, so she missed by a bristle.

A stream of what sounded like curses burst from the filthy storm. "Schmecktenfrettle! Borging skell and blicking fritch!"

"I don't know what that means," Patience hefted her broom, "but you'd better take it back."

The storm tossed several day-old fish at her, which she nimbly dodged. They struck the door behind her — one, two, three. They stuck there a second, then slid down, leaving stinky, glistening trails of guts and scales.

Patience wrinkled her nose.

"You'll have to throw better than that to hit me."

She stamped her foot. She turned to the side. She squared her hips. She stuck out her chin and took a big swing at the strange whirling thing.

Her broom head connected with a soft melon on an updraft. The fruit flew across the alley and splattered all over the wall of the building next door.

A quivering ball of creamy noodles shot back at her. Patience dropped to the ground. Even so, some curdled noodle-cream splashed down the back of her neck. Seizing the high ground, the whirlwind bore straight down on her. It sputtered the most awful, unrepeatable things. She rolled out of the way, over several nasty lumps of squishy ick. She twisted her legs under her and sprung up. She brandished her broom.

"Oi! Come on then!"

The trash-storm reversed course. It fired a barrage of wet chicken bones as it charged. Patience knocked the bones out of the air one after another. She stepped out of the whirlwind's path. The wind fluttered the hem of her skirt as it passed. She set herself firm. She drew the broom back as far as it would go and whacked the cursing garbage right in its middle as hard as she could.

This time, instead of a piece of trash, she hit something far more solid. The wind stopped cursing mid-curse. Every bit of garbage in the air dropped to the ground. A tiny filthy man, who till that moment had been invisible, appeared where the whirlwind had been. He rolled head over heels across the alley. He bounced off the brick wall of *The Crock and Dice* and fell face down in a puddle of sour milk and mustard.

He lay there and did not move.

"Oh dear!" Patience exclaimed.

She peered at the unpleasant little man. She reached out the bristle-end of the broom as far as it would go, until she could poke him. He did not react. She prodded him again, more firmly. He lay as still as a sack of wet barley. She worked the handle tip underneath him and flipped his limp body over.

"Are you dead?"

She had to laugh when she heard herself say that. Of course he wasn't dead. She hadn't hit him *that* hard.

Still, he wasn't moving. Concerned, she stepped closer. She pulled her collar up over her nose and mouth. He smelled like the largest cowpie ever, steaming all summer day long in the sun, packed down into a space the size of a mangy alley cat.

"Sir? Hello?"

Still nothing. Worrisome. He clearly needed her help. She took as deep a breath as she dared through the sturdy fabric of her dress and bent down to investigate. She heard a faint wheezing sound from his crusty lips.

"Well, that's good," she said with some relief. "Now let's see about getting you inside."

She checked around the alley for something she could use to scrape him off the cobbles without touching him. Before she could do that, he leapt suddenly to his feet. Panic seized his face.

"Dreck and drettle!" He scuttled into a drain pipe and was gone.

Out in the street, the townsfolk kept rushing by. No one seemed to have seen the weird whirlwind fight.

****

Fox in a bonnet! Something's afoot in Whosebourne and Patience Fell's just the person to figure out what. Read her story in one of Kirkus Reviews' Best Books of 2020.

The Chaos Court *is available now, everywhere books are sold.*

9 781734 664249